Hidden Treasures:

Switched

By Shiloh Sanders

Hidden Treasures: Switched
Copyright © 2010 by Shiloh Sanders

SandStarr Publications
2422 N Samson Way, Suite 3D
Waukegan, IL 60087

This is a work of fiction. Names, characters, places, and events either are the product of the author's imagination or are used fictitiously.

ISBN 10: 0-9826-6972-0
ISBN 13: 978-0-982-66972-3

Front cover art and layout design by Starr Sanders
Back cover art and layout design by Brad Gomes

Dedications

This is for my family: Pamela Mason Shadell, Derrick Sanders, Bobby Shadell, Alethia Sanders, Errika Sanders, Zachary Andrew, Derrick T. Sanders, Robert Shadell, Sharon Sanders, Grandma Martha Mason, and the rest of the Mason/Sanders/Shadell family.

This is for my friends: Jacob Carlson, Edwina McCollum, Onika Lowe, Jenny Watkins, Leslie Watkins, Nikki Watkins, Jannifer Fuller, Brandy Fuller, R.J. Fuller, Wendy Patterson, Steve Patterson, Candace Patterson, Maritza Pratt, Francisco Cantoran, Scott Armstrong, Deanna Tappy, Matt Kimmeth, Alex Deans, Aaron Jacobs, Karl Spaeth, Joey Waters, Xavier Johnson, Thea Mathis, Halquin Mason, Sheridia Mason, and Atria Mason.

This is for all of the teachers that I've ever had, especially my former English teachers: Mrs. K. Rinehart, Mrs. Hoffman, Mr. Renton, Mr. Ramlose, Mr. Tennant, Mr. Donahue, Mrs. Tantengco, and Mr. Frank Walker.

And last but not least, this is for Zion (go ZeeBees), Illinois, and the surrounding suburbs: Beach Park, Zion, Waukegan, North Chicago, Winthrop Harbor, and Arlington Heights.

This is for my little sisters (Errika and Alethia),
My little brothers (Bobby and Derrick),
My god-sisters (Onika Lowe and Jannifer Fuller),
My surrogate little brother (Joey Costa),
And my surrogate little sister (Luisa Villegas)
Love you guys!

Hidden Treasures:

Switched

*part *one
*patty

prologue

They say that high school years are supposed to be the best years of your life. High school is a phase of your life when you should be the most carefree, when you should be having the most fun. Adults say that after high school, the rest of your life is supposed to go downhill.

I'm a junior in high school and the fun hasn't started yet for me. Is that normal? Most of the other juniors and seniors seem to be having a blast, but I hate having to get up early every morning. I hate having to stand in front of my closet and debate on what I'm going to wear to school. Would I get made fun of more if I wore this pink angora sweater, or would I get made fun of more if I wore my knee-length denim jumper? After that debate, there were still other things to worry about: how to style my hair, how I should wear my backpack, and whether or not I should try putting on some makeup.

I don't know why it takes so long for me to get ready in the morning, because no matter what clothes I put on, how I style my hair, or what makeup I wear, the results are always the same. The boys in school, and even some of the girls, still make fun of me.

I could walk into school dressed in clothes off of a designer rack with my hair professionally styled by one of the best hair stylists, and I would still be made fun of. Why?

Because I'm not a walking, talking, *breathing* toothpick, that's why. I'm just Patricia Coben, a junior who attends Vista Heights High School in a small suburb of Cleveland, Ohio. I have shoulder-length dark blonde hair and bright

1

blue eyes. If someone asked me what I thought my best feature was, I'd definitely say that my eyes were my best feature. They're almond-shaped, the color of sapphires, and fringed by thick, blonde lashes. *Slender* isn't a word that I would use to describe myself, because I'm not slender at all. I'm actually a little on the heavy side. I always have been ever since I was a kid. It's something that I've grown to accept, and believe me-I've heard it all.

When I was a kid, the little boys would gather around me in a circle and sing, "Patty, Patty, you're a fatty." That was when I was in elementary school. When I was in junior high school, I was called everything that you could think of, from "Big Foot," to "Sasquatch," and from "Hungry, Hungry, Hippo," to "Fatty Patty."

In high school, a lot of the ridicule seemed to scale down a bit. My classmates seemed to be a little more accepting of me, because by the time I'd reached freshman year of high school, I'd had a wonderful personality and disposition that couldn't be dismissed.

I really don't mean to make my life sound so horrible. It wasn't always the pits. I acquired a great group of friends, and I even have a boyfriend now. My boyfriend's name is Ricky Kellerman. We've been dating now for almost two years, since the end of freshman year.

I think Ricky has been a big part of why a lot of the jokes and name-calling died down, because Ricky doesn't tolerate a lot of that nonsense.

It does seem, though, that recently some of the name-calling has started again. I'm not sure why. I'm not even sure I care. I've grown accustomed to being made fun of. It doesn't bother me anymore. It sure does bother Ricky, though.

chapter one

I was having a bad day. It began when I was late for the bus in the morning. I had to call a cab and it took the cab about a half hour to show up, so I was *still* late to school even after all of that trouble. When you're late to class at our school, unless you have a valid reason for being late, you have to sit in an in-school detention session in what serves as our school's cafeteria. For this reason, a lot of students abuse in-school detention as an excuse to ditch certain classes that they don't want to attend on any given day.

In-school detention is a lot like a study hall, where you're supposed to use the time to study or complete class assignments. I did neither. I merely stared out of the cafeteria windows and daydreamed.

It seemed that I'd only been there for five or ten minutes when the bell signaling the end of the period shrilled. I scrambled to my feet and collided with Tabatha Andrews in the process.

Her mouth twisted in disgust and she shrank away from me. "Watch where you're going," she snapped, tossing her ebony hair over one shoulder and staring daggers at me.

"I'm sorry," I was quick to apologize. It was a wonder I'd been able to get any words out at all. I was frozen where I stood; I could only look at her in awe, no matter how nasty and cold she was being to me.

That's the way it was with Tabatha Andrews. She was the prettiest, most popular girl in school. She had dark eyes, dark hair that hung down her back, and a year-round tan that wasn't courtesy of the tanning salon down the street. If it

3

wasn't for all of the makeup she caked on her face, she would have looked like a Native American princess. Instead, she looked like exactly what she happened to be: the captain of the cheerleading squad here at Vista Heights High. She was also extremely intelligent and dated the most popular boy at school, Zander Davis.

She dismissed my apology with a wave of her hand. A mob of other girls swarmed around her. They were also cheerleaders, although I often had trouble remembering their names. I was always mixing them up because they all looked alike to me. With the exception of Tabatha, they all had bleached blonde hair and matching tanning salon tans that gave their skin a pumpkin orange tint. They all walked alike, talked alike, and dressed alike. They might as well have been septuplets.

And they all chattered away without acknowledging me at all.

Tabatha started moving with them, listening intently to what they had to say. Then, without warning, she stopped walking and cast a glance over her shoulder, looking directly at me. Her mouth twisted into a smirk again and she said to one of the blonde clones, "If I ever get that fat, Shelly, just kill me. End my misery."

The other girls turned and eyed me up and down, acknowledging my presence for the first time. Then they all erupted into an explosion of giggles.

"I'm not fat!" I shouted at their backs. "I'm big-boned!"

I watched their departure. Strangely enough, I wasn't offended by Tabatha's comment. As I said before, I've pretty much heard it all. Granted, the words had a lot more weight to them since they'd come from Tabatha Andrews herself, the self-proclaimed Queen of Vista Heights High. Queen or not, it would take a lot more than her to ruin the rest of my day.

And it did.

After last period, I waited for Ricky at his locker. It was a daily ritual; we always met by his locker after school. He usually offered to give me a ride home so that I wouldn't have to take the bus.

He took longer than usual to reach his locker. When he saw me, I could see the hesitation in his eyes. He approached me slowly, running a hand through his greasy brown hair. "Hi," he said.

"Hi," I returned awkwardly. There was an odd tension in the air, and I didn't know why it was there.

He looked at me for a moment before saying, "I can't do this anymore."

"Can't do *what* anymore?" I asked, even though I already knew the answer.

"This. Us."

"Oh."

Without explaining himself, he twisted the knob on his locker and entered the combination before pulling the door open and heaving some of his books inside.

I watched the act without budging from my spot. My feet seemed to have been rooted to the floor somehow.

He closed the locker and looked at me again. He wasn't an unattractive boy. He was actually very nice-looking, and could be even *more* nice-looking if he tried. His dark brown hair was curly and always looked greasy. Acne pock marks littered his cheeks. He was tall and lanky; he was often called "Lurch" by his friends. Even though he had these qualities that automatically disqualified him for being traditionally beautiful, I still often thought that he was too good-looking for me. I don't know why.

I guess he woke up and realized this as well. He kept running his hand through his hair and sneaking looks at me out the corners of his eyes. I crossed my arms over my overdeveloped chest and said, "I guess you're not going to give me a reason."

"I don't even know if there is a reason," he mumbled. "I just don't want to be tied down right now."

"Okay," I said. "That's all you had to say."

He looked surprised. "Really?"

"Yeah."

He almost smiled, but stopped himself for some reason. I guess he didn't want to look too giddy that he'd gotten off the hook. "So...we can still be friends, then?"

"No."

"No?"

I shook my head. "No, we can't be friends. But maybe I'll wave to you once in awhile."

He looked disheartened, but instead of dwelling on the negative, he seemed to focus on the fact that he no longer had to be "tied down." He gave me a sheepish wave and jogged towards one of the school's exits.

I watched him with a heavy feeling in my heart. I'm proud of myself, though. I didn't cry. Not at first. I numbly turned and exited the school, boarded the school bus, and collapsed on the nearest empty seat.

One of my best friends, Dana Myers, called me later that night. I didn't tell her right away what had happened between Ricky and me, but she could tell by the tone of my voice that something was wrong.

When I finally did tell her what had happened, she told me, "He didn't deserve you anyway. Are you kidding me?"

"I think I'm just frustrated that he didn't tell me why he was breaking up with me," I mumbled, wiping at the tears that were rolling down my cheeks. I was perched on the edge of my bed in flannel pajamas. I'd turned off the lights in my room, so I was sitting in complete darkness.

"He's an idiot and you're better off without him," Dana insisted.

She was always talking about how boys were stupid and nowhere near as smart as girls were. She'd only had one boyfriend that I knew of, and his name had been Johnny Wade. She and Johnny had lasted a couple of months before she caught him holding hands with another girl. A couple of days later both of the wheels on Johnny's bike were flat due to twin punctures. Dana had never owned up to it.

She was probably right in saying that I was better off without Ricky, but for some reason I couldn't stop thinking about him.

"Don't worry," she assured me before we both hung up. "Tomorrow will be a better day than today was."

The next day wasn't any better. Because of the break-up, I wasn't my usual upbeat self. I robotically walked up and down the halls like a brain-dead zombie. Some of my friends later told me that they'd shouted greetings to me, but I hadn't heard them. I had been in my own little world, a world without Ricky.

In gym class, the juniors had to play the seniors in a game of volleyball. I can only imagine how glassy-eyed I looked. I never made a move for the ball. Soon, my teammates were shouting at me.

"Go for the ball, fatty!"

"That was all you, Patty."

"If you jump into the air, you won't get stuck, Patty. I promise."

I could clearly see Tabatha standing on the other side of the net. She was next in line to serve. She snickered at something one of her teammates said and tossed the ball into the air for an overhand serve. The ball soared over the net and smacked me…

…*Right* in the face. I teetered backwards and crashed to the floor. I don't know how long I was unconscious. All I know is that when I came to, a sea of faces hovered over me. The face that was most noticeable, of course, belonged to Tabatha. She had her hand on my forehead, as if checking for a fever or something. I swatted at her hand. "Don't touch me," I told her coldly. "I don't have a fever. You hit me with the volleyball. I'm not sick."

Tabatha straightened into a standing position. "I was just trying to see if you were all right."

"I'm fine."

The gym teacher, Mrs. Prescott, came jogging our way with the school nurse in tow. Mrs. Prescott looked relieved that I'd gained consciousness.

I struggled to my feet and all the while, my classmates were making snide comments about my thick thighs and the small tummy that protruded slightly over my gym shorts. If Mrs. Prescott hadn't been there, I probably would have flipped them all the bird. I suppressed the urge and instead, headed to the locker room.

It didn't take long for the rest of the class to trickle in after me, and I couldn't help but hear some of their comments.

"When she fell, I could have sworn that the whole floor shook!"

"That's what happens when you eat carbs. That's why I *never* eat carbs."

"Nice serve, Tabby."

"I just couldn't bear it if I ever got that big."

That last comment was the undoing of me. I rounded the corner and directed to Shelly Woods, the commenter, "Believe me, Shelly. There are worse things in the world than being fat."

"Really?" Shelly questioned, half-serious. "Like what?"

"Cancer, for one," I said, advancing on her. "Tumors. Diseases. Infections."

She tilted her nose in the air, tossing her straight blonde hair in the process. "I guess," she admitted. "I guess those things are worse than being fat. But allowing yourself to look like that just shows that you don't care about yourself. If you did, you would start working out. Or get liposuction. Or something."

I drew my hand back, intent on smacking her across the face. But someone grabbed my closed fist and kept me from completing the task. With my fist suspended in midair, I whirled around to face Tabatha.

"Violence isn't the answer," Tabatha said smoothly, walking past me and setting an arm across Shelly's shoulders. "She's just showing her concern for you."

"She's not *concerned* about me," I shouted. "None of you are."

"Don't be so hostile, Patty," Tabatha continued in a calm tone of voice.

"Are you getting a pimple on your nose?" I asked instead of responding. I leaned closer to Tabatha, as if inspecting her nose.

She timidly brought a hand up to her nose and pressed an index finger to the tip of it. "You see a pimple?" she asked worriedly. "Oh my God. Do you really?" She turned and ran for the bathroom so that she could check her reflection.

I didn't wait for her to return. I hastily grabbed my belongings and left the locker room, even though I was still dressed in my gym uniform.

The story hit the school like wildfire. Everyone heard about what had happened in gym class between Tabatha and me. I'm sure she was spreading a lot of the gossip around herself. No one believed that I had the audacity to go up against the most popular girl in school. After all, who was Patricia Coben? As far as most of the student body was concerned, I was a nobody. I didn't have the status that Tabatha did. I didn't have the fashion sense that she did and my family definitely didn't have the money that hers did. No one considered me as being in the same league as Tabatha. I didn't even consider *myself* in the same league as her.

Did I think that she was a better person than I was? No. Did I think that she was prettier than I was? I'm not sure. It depends on what pretty means to you. Tabatha was thin and had traditionally pretty features. She could be a model if she wanted to be, I'm sure. Was I traditionally pretty? No, not by a long shot.

But when I looked in the mirror, and I did a lot after that encounter with Tabatha and Shelly, the face that looked back at me wasn't ugly. The face that looked back at me was cute. The body attached to the face wasn't one that would be gracing the cover of *Seventeen* magazine anytime soon, but I was okay with that. I was still beautiful to myself, regardless of that fact.

Whether I thought I was beautiful or not, the following weeks were horrible. It seemed that Tabatha had declared a personal vendetta against me for embarrassing her in the locker room. Whenever she was within earshot of me, she always had something negative to say about me, the way I looked, and the clothes that I wore.

"Would it *kill* you to wear something cute for once?"

"Who wears thick stockings anymore? I mean really?"

"No one over the age of ten years old should wear pig tails, Patty. I mean really."

Most of the time, I held in my retorts. Usually Tabatha was surrounded by her cronies, her annoying circle of friends and her boyfriend, Zander.

While her friends sometimes chimed in, Zander never did. He glanced at me once in awhile, but was always quiet whenever Tabatha started one of her verbally abusive rants.

While Mary Blume, one of my friends, held in her negative comments regarding Tabatha, Dana openly despised Tabatha. Dana didn't care who heard what she had to say. She had a couple of choice words for the cheerleading captain and didn't care for the way I was being treated.

My parents were too self-involved to realize what I was going through. They never showed an interest in my daily activities. They rarely asked how my day was at school. If they *had* asked, I would have been blatantly honest with them.

"Well, Mom, Ricky dumped me a few weeks ago because he finally woke up and realized I'm a fat, ugly cow. I still haven't gotten over that. As if that weren't enough, Tabatha Andrews is now making my life a living hell because I embarrassed her in front of a group of nosey girls. How was your day at work?"

I could just imagine myself saying something like that to my mother. It probably wouldn't have shocked her at all. She probably would have tilted her head to the side and told me how her day had been.

Adults often forget just how cruel adolescents can be. They dress you up when you're five years old and send you off to school with the promise that it'll be the most fun you've ever had. "You'll get to know other little kids, and you'll have so much fun learning your ABC's and 123's!" And to their credit, at first school *is* fun.

At first, you're running around and playing Hide and Seek and Duck, Duck, Goose, and there's nothing more fun in the world than to jump up in the morning and get dressed for school.

And then once you've left elementary school, things change. Those darned preteens creep up on everybody and all of a sudden the little boys only care about video games and poking animals with sticks and the little girls care about the little boys. From that point, everything becomes tainted with vanity and pop culture.

There was one particular day when all of the emotions that I'd suppressed caught up to me. I stumbled into a wall of lockers at the end of the school day. The halls were empty and silent. I'd been walking towards the school exit so that I could board the school bus and head home, but I didn't make it quite that far. I fell against the row of lockers and slid down to the floor.

A wave of emotion just hit me, and flashbacks of the past few weeks flickered behind my eyes. Tears started rolling down my cheeks and I wiped at them in vain. More of them kept coming. Through the veil of tears, I could see someone approaching me. Someone was asking if I was all right. Did I *look* all right?

He pulled me to my feet and pulled me against him. I still didn't know who my knight in shining armor was. I just buried my face in his chest and cried.

The sound of approaching footsteps drew near and a feminine voice demanded, "Zander, what do you think you're doing?"

I quickly wiped away my tears and looked up into the face of Zander Davis. His dark brown hair brushed his shoulders as he lifted his emerald green eyes to meet those of the girl who'd interrupted us. I shifted my gaze in the direction of the female voice that I'd heard and of course, the voice belonged to none other than Tabatha Andrews herself. And boy, did she look annoyed to see me in the arms of her boyfriend.

chapter two

"I asked you a question, Zander."

His arm stayed around me. He didn't budge from where he was standing, and for that I was thankful. "She wasn't feeling so well," he answered after a moment. "I just wanted to make sure she was okay."

"She's a nobody!" Tabatha yelled. Her voice bounced off of the linoleum floors and off of the walls. "Why would you care how she feels?"

"She looked sad," he said. "I couldn't just walk right past her without seeing how she was doing."

I pulled away from him and stood on my own. "I feel better," I muttered, not wanting to get between the popular couple. "But thanks so much for...for everything."

I walked away from them, but not before hearing Tabatha mimic, "Thanks for '*everything*'? What's that supposed to mean, Zander? Huh?"

If I had felt any better, I would have laughed at that. The old Patricia Coben would have had a field day with that entire scenario. But I didn't feel like myself at all. I felt beaten down and defeated.

It didn't take me long to realize that I'd missed my bus, which only left me the option of walking home. My house wasn't that far from school, and the day was warm and sunny, so instead of trying to catch a ride with one of my other schoolmates, I started walking in the general direction of my house.

I walked past several familiar stores and came to stop in front of an unfamiliar one. The name etched into the sign was Hidden Treasures, but the only items on display were a couple of old-looking books and unrecognizable goop in an assortment of jars. There was a large, crimson banner advertising the store's grand opening tomorrow.

Someone lightly tapped my shoulder and I whirled around, coming face-to-face with Tabatha.

"I'm beginning to think you have a crush on me," I said even though I wasn't in the mood for joking around.

Neither was she. She wrinkled her nose in disgust and tossed her dark hair over one shoulder. "I just came to give you a warning," she told me.

I couldn't help but arch a brow. "What warning is that?"

"To stay away from Zander," she replied. "I don't know why he concerned himself with an oinker like you anyway, but he's my boyfriend. So hands off."

I didn't get the chance to think of something clever to say in response to that, because after saying those words, she turned and strutted down the sidewalk.

I could only stand there, a prisoner of my own rage.

"I'm going to guess that the two of you aren't friends," said a low, silky voice.

I turned to face a tall, slender figure standing in the doorway of the Hidden Treasures shop. The door stood propped open, allowing me a limited view of the shop itself.

"Maybe it's none of my business," the person said, shrugging. I couldn't tell if it was a man or a woman. Platinum blonde hair hung down to the shoulders and the eyes that were sizing me up were the brightest shade of blue I'd ever seen.

"No, she and I aren't friends," I confessed. "We're quite the opposite."

"Hidden Treasures may be of service to you, then."

I looked over at the display window and shook my head. "I don't think anyone can help me."

"I'm sure that I can," the store owner said confidently.

I followed the store owner into the store. I don't know why. There was a small amount of hope burning within me, hope that this store could somehow solve all of my problems.

"My name is Aidan Powers," the store owner explained. "The store's grand opening is tomorrow, but I've had a couple of people stop into the store today, curious as to what I'm selling."

"What *do* you sell?" I asked curiously. I couldn't stop myself.

"I sell dreams," Aidan answered. With his deep voice and broad shoulders, I assumed that he was a man. I still wasn't absolutely sure because even though he had a deep voice and a muscular build, the graceful way in which he moved looked feminine to me.

"How can you sell dreams?" I asked as we walked through the aisles of the store.

He shrugged in response to the question, but stopped and reached out to one of the shelves, grabbing one of the bottles. "For example, would you believe that the contents of this bottle could make you into a rock star?"

"No," I said honestly. "I couldn't believe something like that."

"Of course not," he said, returning the bottle to its place and moving along. "We stop believing in the supernatural when we become a certain age. We're told that the Tooth Fairy and Santa Clause don't exist, so nothing else magical exists, either."

"Are you claiming that you sell magic?" I asked.

He turned and looked down at me. "I told you," he said. "I sell dreams. You can call it magic. You can call it tricks. You can call it whatever you wish to call it, but in essence, I sell dreams."

I considered turning and running out of the store. After all, Aidan Powers was still technically a stranger, whether or not he'd introduced himself to me. He could be a complete whacko.

He tilted his head back and laughed. "If you wish to turn and run, then do so," he told me. "I'm not going to force you to stay here."

I hadn't voiced my thoughts aloud, had I? I was sure that I hadn't, and yet he'd known exactly what I'd been thinking. Without a word, he turned and continued down the aisle. After giving it a moment's thought, I followed him further into the store.

He sent me home with a small pamphlet that could have been the Cliff's Notes to *Julius Caesar*. There was no cover art or text on the front cover of the pamphlet. It looked plain and inexpensive. I didn't open the book, not yet. He'd told me that he was sure that it was what I needed, so I took it with me. When I dug into my pockets to dig out the few crumpled dollar bills that I had, he refused them.

"This one is free of charge," he said with a mysterious smile on his face. "The only thing that you want to keep in mind is that even though this will aid in making your dreams come true, you are not to use anything from this store with malicious intent."

Okay, I could deal with that. Supposedly this pamphlet was going to solve all of my problems *and* it was free?

As soon as I got home, I tossed the pamphlet into my desk dresser. I got some of my homework out of the way, went downstairs when my mother called me down to dinner, and all the while the pamphlet was still on my mind.

My mother looked concerned. She was a short, slender woman with blonde hair and green eyes. If she gained another fifty pounds, she'd probably look exactly like me. Her brows were currently wrinkled with worry. "Are you all right?" she asked me.

"I'm fine," I said before shoveling a spoonful of mashed potatoes into my mouth.

She continued to stare at me.

My little brother Brendon was oblivious to it all, forking roast beef and spinach into his mouth. He always saved the mashed potatoes for last so that he could play with it and form it into forts and mountains and whatever else he shaped his food into.

My mother changed the topic when she realized that I wasn't going to shed light on anything. She rarely seemed concerned for my well-being. I know that sounds cold, but I was shocked she even noticed that I wasn't feeling well. It's probably because I usually crack jokes at dinner and I wasn't that night.

After dinner, I returned to my room and I finally pulled my desk drawer open and pulled out the pamphlet. I jumped on my bed with it and opened the front cover. The first page was blank. Confused, I flipped to the second page, which was also blank. I thumbed through the entire book, only to find out that all of the pages in the book were blank.

No wonder he gave it to me for free, I thought to myself. *It's nothing but blank sheets of paper!* This was what was supposed to solve all of my problems? An empty book?

Angrily, I shoved the book into my backpack. Was this some sort of practical joke or prank? Was this some sort of gimmick to get me to go back to the store the next day for the grand opening? Whatever it was, I was going to take the book back to the store. I didn't deserve to be conned like that.

I turned off the lights in my room and fell into a restless sleep. My dreams are usually my escape from the torment of the real world, but that night, I didn't have a dream. I had a nightmare.

I was standing very close to a boy with light brown hair and he had his arms wrapped tightly around me. The boy happened to be Zander. So far, so good.

He was hugging me and holding on to me and whispering sweet nothings in my ear. "Everything's going to be okay," he was saying. "You don't have to worry about a thing. I don't want to be with Tabatha. I haven't wanted to be with her for a long time. I want to be with you, Patty. Only you."

I looked up at him and he looked down at me. We were seconds away from kissing when the school entrance doors blew open. Tabatha stood with sunlight blazing at her back. She stalked down the hall and pulled me away from Zander.

The two of us started to fight. We were rolling around the floor like little kids, tugging at each other's hair and slapping each other. I somehow got on top of her. I started bashing her head into the floor, yanking her head up by her hair and smashing it back down into the floor. All of my anger bubbled to the surface and before long, my hands were covered in blood and Tabatha's face was almost unrecognizable.

I stood up from the carnage and looked down. Zander came to stand at my back. He drew his arms around my waist and pulled me to him. "You see?" he asked me. "I told you everything would be all right. Now we don't have to worry about her anymore. It's just you and me."

I bolted upright in bed and glanced around my room. Nothing looked out of place. I don't know why I expected anything to be out of place. I could feel beads of sweat on my forehead. I could still remember the nightmare, quite clearly, as if it were something that had happened in real life. But that was silly. That hadn't happened yesterday. The scene back at school had gone differently. I hadn't beaten Tabatha into a bloody pulp. Zander hadn't told me that he wanted to be with me. All of that was a figment of my imagination.

I rolled over on my side and saw the pamphlet peeking out of my backpack. A sliver of moonlight beamed into my room from the window behind my desk. The light illuminated the pamphlet so that it appeared to be glowing.

I shivered beneath my flower-print comforter and sat up on my elbows. I could hear a distinct tapping sound, but that was most likely just the tree branch tapping against my window. It made that sound sometimes. I don't know why I was so jumpy.

My eyes kept drifting over to the pamphlet. It still appeared to be glowing. I stood out of bed, walked across my room, and knelt down to the floor. I pulled the book out of my backpack and went back over to my bed, where I leaned over my nightstand and flicked on the lamp.

I opened the front page. I must have expected to see something different, because I'd walked across my room to get the book. Still, I didn't expect to see what I did. Because written on the first page of the book, in my handwriting, was a single step:

step 1: Obtain a strand of her hair

I closed the book with my brows furrowed. I'd looked at this book earlier tonight and there hadn't been anything printed in it. How was it that there were words in this book now? And how was it possible that the text was in my own sloppy handwriting?

I couldn't make any sense of what the words were supposed to mean. Obtain a strand of *whose* hair?

chapter three

The following day was Thursday. Nothing interesting happened during the school day. I bumped into Ricky during lunch period, quite literally. He'd apologized and had moved away from me before I could say anything.

The old me would have thought of a way to get Ricky back. After all, we'd been dating for almost two years. He probably still had feelings for me. There had to be some other reason that had caused him to break up with me.

The truth was, though, that I didn't want Ricky back. Even when he and I were dating, I'd known that I wasn't in love with him or anything. He and I had fun whenever we hung out and it was fun having someone to go to the movies with. He wasn't the love of my life. I was probably too young to recognize the love of my life whenever it approached me.

I walked into the courtyard with my lunch tray and sat on a bench. I lowered the tray onto the bench next to me. Birds were twittering in the trees and a gentle breeze blew across the courtyard. The day was truly beautiful. It was amazing really, how people were confined to be traditionally or untraditionally beautiful, whereas nature was just purely beautiful. Nature *was* beauty.

I was so tied up in my thoughts that I didn't realize that Zander was purposely striding towards me until he took a seat next to me on the bench.

I nearly choked on my piece of sandwich. Was he *trying* to make Tabatha angry with me? Was that why he kept coming around?

"It's a pretty day, isn't it?" he asked in a casual tone.

I narrowed my eyes at him. "It is," I answered.

"I've always loved the courtyard. It's probably the only place in this entire school where I can be myself."

"You should be able to be yourself anywhere," I muttered, glancing around us.

He shrugged his shoulders. "I should be able to, but I'm not. Everywhere else, I'm expected to be someone else. On the football field, I'm expected to be a wonderful athlete, the next best thing since Tom Brady. In the classroom, I'm expected to have a passion for mathematical equations and English literature, when I couldn't care less about either." He braced his hands on the back of the bench and leaned backward. "The truth is, I'd rather just sit here and exist. Appreciate what's around me. I don't know."

"I know what you mean," I said cautiously. "We have to wear a lot of faces when we're at school."

"It won't change when we grow up," he said. "When we're adults, we'll have jobs and we'll be forced into being someone else for eight hours each day."

I couldn't help but stare at him. I would have never guessed that he had such deep, intense thoughts. I was too stunned to speak. I simply nodded in agreement and stared at the trees.

Several times, I felt his eyes on me but I was too chicken to look back. He was sitting next to me and he didn't care who saw us sitting together. He was talking to me like a real person, without caring about our social status or what I looked like.

He sighed and stood up. "I guess no matter what age we are, we'll always have to perform for everyone else at some point or another."

"We don't *have* to," I said suddenly, standing up also. "If we wanted to, we could just be ourselves whenever we wanted to. Who cares about what someone else wants us to be?"

A faint smile touched his lips. I'd rarely seen his smile, but he had a beautiful one. "Maybe you're right," he said, backing away from me.

I said to his retreating back, "And maybe we don't have to date the head cheerleader just because it's a popular trend for the football quarterback to date the cheerleading captain."

He paused in his stride, turned and looked at me over his shoulder. The look in his eyes was startling and intense. "Maybe you're right," he said again.

At the end of the day, I was at my locker putting some of my schoolbooks into my bag when I heard someone shout, "Fatty Patty!"

I knew who the voice belonged to without turning around. I turned around anyway.

Tabatha stood at the end of the hallway with her hands planted on her hips. She was wearing a tight shirt the color of violets and a short, black skirt. Most girls who wore skirts that short to school were sent home or had to wear their gym uniform for the remainder of the school day but when you were Tabatha Andrews and owned the school, I guess you didn't have to worry about things like that.

Her eyes spit fire at me as she charged towards me.

I stood at my locker without budging an inch, wondering what she wanted with me *now*.

"I heard you were in the courtyard with Zander during lunch," she said through gritted teeth.

I rolled my eyes. Was *that* what this was about?

"Is it true?" she asked me. She'd finally reached me.

I looked straight into her eyes. "Yes, we both had lunch in the courtyard."

Tabatha threw her head back and laughed. "Are you really trying to steal my boyfriend, Patty? Do you seriously think that he would want to date *you*? *You* of all people?"

"I'm not trying to steal anyone's boyfriend," I said evenly. "We were just having lunch."

"I thought I told you to stay away from him."

"I don't obey your orders, Tabatha. You may own everyone else in this school, but you don't own me." I thought about my next words before saying them. I took a moment to consider the consequences. I'd probably make her a lot angrier, but you know what? I didn't care. I squared my chin, tilted my nose up, and continued, "Obviously you don't own Zander either."

She let out the most furious shriek I'd ever heard and pounced on me. She grabbed my throat and squeezed. I reached my hands up and pulled on her hair.

She screamed in pain and leapt back, giving me the time and opportunity to jump on her and knock her to the ground. Soon, we were rolling around on the floor. She smacked me hard in the face and I slapped her back. Then I grabbed her by her hair and made as if to slam her head into the floor. Somehow, this was all familiar to me.

She was still clawing at me and I paused, with her hair wrapped around my hand. I wasn't going to bash her head in. I couldn't. I didn't want to hurt her, not that badly. I just wanted to show her that I wasn't someone to mess around with.

I abruptly let her head go. And her head smacked hard on the floor. Her eyes closed and she turned her head to the side. I jumped to my feet, frightened. She wasn't dead, was she? I should probably take her pulse or something. But what if she was just playing a trick, waiting for me to get close so that she could hurt me?

I stood there, debating what I should do, when the words from the pamphlet came back to me.

Step 1: Obtain a strand of her hair

I looked down at my hands. Several strands of Tabatha's hair were wrapped around my fingers. I already had her hair in the palms of my hands. I dropped to the floor in front of my locker, where I'd left my backpack, and slid the strands of hair in the pamphlet. Then, I shut my locker, slung my backpack over my shoulder, and ran out of the school doors without so much as glancing over my shoulder.

That night, I had another nightmare.

Tabatha and I were still fighting in the hallway. I pulled on her hair and held her head up, but I hesitated. I didn't want Tabatha to be hurt. I just wanted her to leave me alone from now on. I wanted her to stop picking on me. That's all I wanted.

Zander materialized in the hallway, and he had an evil grin on his face. "Why are you hesitating?" he asked me. "Don't you want to be with me?"

I looked up at him, confused. "Yes," I answered. "I mean, I think so."

"You think so? You don't know whether or not you want to be with me?"

"I mean…" I shook my head left, then right. "I mean, of course I want to be with you."

"For you to be with me, we have to get rid of her," he said with a look of distaste. He nodded his head in Tabatha's direction.

Tabatha twisted and turned in my grasp, but I was on top of her. She couldn't move, not with me holding her down. "Let me go!" she screamed.

"As long as she's around, we won't get the chance to be together," Zander continued, kneeling down to the floor, only a few feet away from Tabatha and me. "She'll always be on our case, always in our faces. You know it's true."

"But I can't hurt her," I said helplessly. "I'm not a killer. I don't want to kill her."

One moment, he was a few feet away and the next, he was behind me, whispering roughly into my ear, "Yes you do. Be honest with yourself."

My mouth dropped open. "No," I whispered.

"Yes," he said persuasively. "Do it. Do it for you and me. Do it so that we can be together."

Tabatha was screaming uncontrollably now. "I thought you loved me!" she was shouting at Zander.

"How could I love you?" he asked. "You're arrogant, heartless, and cold. You think the world revolves around you, but it doesn't. It never did. Patty, I'm only going to tell you one more time. Kill her."

Tears were streaming down my face as I pulled Tabatha's head up, then slammed it hard against the floor. I repeated the action until all I was holding in my hands was what was left of her hair. The back of her head had caved in and a pool of blood was spreading out around us.

Zander had a satisfied smile on his face as he grabbed my hands and helped me up. "See? Now we can be together, Patty," he said to me, brushing his lips against my cheek. "Now, it's just you and me."

I floundered around in my bed, struggling with my sheets and my comforter. I fell off of the bed and landed near my backpack. The nightmare was still fresh in my mind. It gave me the creeps. As cruel as Tabatha was, I would never want to kill her.

I rummaged through my backpack in the dark, and pulled out the pamphlet. I somehow knew that there would be another step printed on the second page, and I was right. I had to scramble back into bed and turn on the lamp, because I couldn't read the text in the dark.

Step 2: embrace your rage

chapter four

I'll be completely honest. I had no clue as to what the second step meant. Embrace my rage? How was I supposed to do that? What would happen once I *did* do it? What were all of these steps leading up to?

I would soon find out what it meant to embrace my rage. The next day was Friday. The day started out the way it usually does. I, a junior, for some reason board a school bus when both of my parents know I should be driving my own car by now. I ride the bus to school, get off the bus (reluctantly), and enter a school that has come to be the bane of my existence.

Then I attend classes that I could really care less about at this point in my life. I pretend I'm paying attention to the teachers, the teachers pretend to care about what I want in life, and everyone is generally happy.

That's how the day *started*, anyway. The day became a runaway train when Tabatha saw Zander and me talking near my locker. Okay, granted I don't know why he keeps talking to me in the first place. Sometimes I think he's weirder than I am. And to Tabatha's credit, she didn't tattletale about the fight we'd had the previous day. I thought that she'd gotten over everything and would leave me alone from then on. I guess I have my moments when I'm an optimist.

But Tabatha blew a gasket when she saw Zander and me talking after fifth period. She marched up to both of us and smacked Zander in the face.

There were students around us and after she slapped Zander, all of their mouths gaped open and the rumor mills started.

The dark-haired cheerleader stood before us, fuming. "I don't care if you're the quarterback, Zander! We're done!" She turned and stalked off, because there really wasn't anything else for her to do, nothing else she could say to either Zander or me.

Zander turned and looked at me and kind of shrugged his shoulders. He didn't seem to care much that his high school romance with Tabatha had just come to a screeching halt. He walked me to my next class and asked if I was doing anything special this weekend. There were a couple of kids within earshot of us. They snickered as they entered the nearest classroom.

I told him that I was available this weekend, but really I was wondering why he was showing so much interest in me. Granted, I'm a funny girl. I know that. I make some jokes that are guaranteed to crack you up. I have a cute face, I'm also aware of that. But I don't dress stylishly. I don't have what boys would call a "killer body." I'm not popular.

Sure, Zander gave the appearance of not caring about that stuff, but was he being genuine? Did he seriously not care about popularity and looks and fancy clothes?

We made a date for Saturday night. I was floating on air when I went home that day. Nothing could have ruined my good mood. Not even my little brother, and that's saying a lot.

I was floating so high, I didn't even pay the pamphlet any heed and I had no nightmares that night. Maybe I didn't need the help of Hidden Treasures after all.

I practically bounced out of bed the next morning. I headed downstairs in my pajama pants and t-shirt. No one else was awake yet; the house was extremely quiet.

I poured myself a bowl of cereal and munched while watching Saturday morning cartoons. I was just about to find out whether or not the Teenage Mutant Ninja Turtles had gotten rid of Shredder for good when my little brother came bounding down the stairs and into the kitchen. He padded into the kitchen in bare feet, rubbing at his eyes with small balled fists. He was only nine years old, but on a good day he could match wits with someone twice his age.

A shock of blonde hair fell over his forehead as he grabbed the cereal from the counter and pulled a clean bowl from the dishwasher.

"Good morning," I greeted, watching him.

"Morning," he returned as he claimed a chair at the kitchen table.

I often felt guilty for not being the big sister that I could have been. I rarely spent time with the little monster otherwise known as Brendon.

We gabbed a bit about cartoons as we watched the cartoon turtles attempt to get the best of a villain with cheese graters for shoulder pads.

My friends came over shortly after that. I hadn't planned to spend the day with them, but they'd heard all of the rumors about me and Zander and they wanted to corner me and ask about all of the gory details.

"We heard that you and Tabatha were fighting over him," Dana accused as soon as she was through the front door. Her long, light brown hair was pulled back in a ponytail.

Mary Blume and Stephanie Foster were close at her heels. Mary closed the door behind her, and in seconds they were all over me.

I fended them off with my hands up. "Hey," I protested. "I'm about as clueless as you guys, all right?"

"How can you be?" Stephanie asked. "You're right in the middle of all of it."

I didn't know how to answer that. "All I know is that Zander has been coming to my defense a lot with Tabatha. She keeps catching us talking and assuming the worst. There isn't anything going on between Zander and me."

"Except that you guys are supposed to be going out tonight," Mary said. "You left that juicy tidbit out."

I couldn't stop myself from blushing. "I'm trying not to get my hopes up," I said. "I don't know what his angle is."

"Why does he have to have an angle?" Dana demanded. "How come he can't just be into you?"

"Because that isn't how it works," I reasoned. "The quarterback doesn't wake up one morning and think to himself that he's always had a crush on the fat girl. Okay?"

Stephanie shrugged her shoulders. "You're such a pessimist."

"It's too weird," I said, even though beneath the surface I was excited and giddy about going out with Zander that night.

I'd been friends with these three girls ever since the fifth grade. Since then, we'd all made subtle changes to our appearances. Mary had dyed her hair from brown to black. Stephanie had dyed her hair from brown to blonde. Dana hadn't dyed her hair, but she'd gotten a lot curvier over the years. I'd simply *grown*. Not curvier, but *bigger*. Wider. A little taller.

"I guess with Zander sniffing after you, Ricky's not even an afterthought for you," Dana said with a grin. Out of all of us, she was the one who still believed that boys had cooties.

"I don't think I'll ever forgive Ricky for what he did to me," I said honestly. "He said that he doesn't want to be tied down right now, but I think there's another reason why he broke up with me. I don't know what the reason could be, but I don't think he was being completely honest with me."

"Who cares?" Mary said dismissively, fishing a piece of gum out of her jeans pocket. "You've got Zander now. Who needs Ricky?"

"We should probably go shopping," Stephanie mused, "to get you a new outfit for your date tonight."

"That's an awesome idea," Dana said, clapping her hands.

I hadn't planned on going shopping, but I guess it couldn't hurt. My wardrobe had seen better days. Dana had driven her car, so we all rode to the mall with her.

They pulled me from store to store, plucking certain pieces of clothing off of the rack and holding it up to me. Vista Heights Mall isn't one of the largest malls I've ever seen; it's not large at all, actually. But there are a lot of decent stores and it's always been an after-school hangout for Vista Heights High students.

We recognized a lot of our classmates as we went from store to store. Some of them waved at us or greeted us. A lot of them didn't. We didn't really care. We were having fun.

Dana tried on a couple of comical outfits and popped out of the dressing room saying, "If we were in a movie, this is where they'd plug in the montage."

I didn't even know what a movie montage was, but I laughed anyway because the outfit that she was wearing looked so ridiculous.

Mary and Stephanie popped out of the dressing rooms on either side of Dana's. They'd entered the store wearing simple cotton tees and jeans, but now they were wearing outfits just as ridiculous as Dana's.

When it was my turn to try something on, I didn't have my friends' attention. They were all staring out of the department store window. I waved my arms in front of their faces. Mary could only raise one solitary index finger and use it to point in the direction in which they were staring.

I followed the direction of their gaze and a damper was immediately put on my happy mood. Zander and Tabatha were strolling down the mall together, hand-in-hand, looking as if they didn't have a care in the world…looking as if Zander didn't have a date with me several hours from now.

All of a sudden, I wasn't in the mood for shopping. I wasn't in the mood for anything except approaching both of them and clocking them in the face. What was he doing with her, anyway? Had he been planning on stringing both of us along?

Dana settled a hand on my shoulder. "Maybe he's just giving the news to her that he'll be going out with you from now on," she said.

I looked down at her. She was the last person who would ever say something nice about a boy. She hated boys, hated what they stood for, and hated the girls that the boys always seemed to be chasing after. She'd never let herself get tricked like this. I shook my head. "No," I said slowly. "He's not giving any news to her. Look at them. They both look happy. He doesn't look like someone who's about to dump her. Believe me…I know what a boy would look like in *that* situation. He looks like a happy-go-lucky guy hanging out with his girlfriend, which is exactly what he's doing."

Mary nervously chewed on the inside of her lip. "What are you going to do?" she asked worriedly.

I don't know why she asked that. Maybe she saw the look that was in my eyes. Maybe the look that she saw was dangerous. Maybe she knew what was going on in my head, because that was even *more* dangerous. I was planning on how I was going to get Tabatha and Zander back. All I could think of were the words that were in the second step: "Embrace your rage." I was doing *just* that.

chapter five

My friends were worried about me. I could tell. They didn't want to leave my side. They wanted to stay with me while I waited for Zander to pick me up. They wanted to let him know what they thought of him, I'm sure. But I couldn't allow that. After all, I knew how to deal with Zander and Tabatha. I wouldn't deal with them at all, as a matter-of-fact. I would let the pamphlet tell me what to do. It seemed to know everything.

Zander was on time. Kudos to him. He was on time and looking as dapper as he always was. He'd even pulled his hair back into a ponytail. As angry as I was with him, I had to be honest. He looked gorgeous. He looked like a Ken doll. If there ever was such a thing as a Backstabber Ken, that is. I don't think they've come out with that model yet. Either way, his eyes lit up when he saw me.

I couldn't help but admire how good of an actor he was. He looked like he was genuinely happy to see me. I let him take my hand in his and he escorted me to his car. His car looked like it cost more than my father made in a year as a call center manager.

The car was small, red, and only had two doors. There was a back seat, but there wasn't much room back there. You'd think that someone with as many friends as he had would want a larger car.

He opened the door for me, waited for me to sit in the passenger seat, and closed the door. Then he jogged around the car to the driver side door. If I hadn't seen what I'd seen earlier today, I would have thought that he was a gentleman. I would have been fooled.

I was thankful to my friends for dragging me to the mall when they had. If they hadn't, I wouldn't have had a clue as to what was going on.

He looked at me long and hard. It took me a moment for me to realize he'd said something to me.

"I'm sorry, what was that?" I asked.

"I was just telling you how pretty you looked."

Liar. "Thank you so much." I was dressed in a fitted, blue shirt and a knee-length black skirt. I hadn't been brave enough to wear a miniskirt, but the knee-length skirt was stylish enough. I'd even worn heels. Almost as an afterthought, I decided to return the compliment. "You look nice too."

He smiled and a dimple deepened into his cheek. "Thanks."

He drove around for awhile and explained that he wanted to go see a movie and then go to dinner, if that was all right with me. "Sure," I said, only half-listening to his words.

If only this night could be real. If only we could really be going on a date together, and fall in love with each other, and show our high school that cliques and status mean nothing. If the high school's fat girl can date the football team's quarterback, then anything was possible. That is what I wanted to show everyone. It looked like I wouldn't get the chance to prove that to them, though. Because it wasn't true at all, was it? Apparently, looks meant everything. It seemed that only the girls that looked like Tabatha Andrews received the happily ever after fairytale ending.

He was looking at me again and I didn't even try to pretend like I cared this time. I continued staring out of the window, almost drowning in my thoughts.

He pulled into the parking lot of the movie theater and played the part of the gentleman again as he opened the door for me and assisted me out of the car. I had the strongest urge to punch him, but I overcame it, thank goodness.

He led me into the theater, where a lot of our classmates were standing at the ticket booth. He held my hand tightly in his. I didn't even know which movie we were supposed to be seeing. When I blinked my eyes, everything that I saw was tinted in red. I had to blink my eyes again to clear them.

"Two tickets for that new action movie," he said to the ticket guy behind the window.

"You really know how to impress a girl," I muttered, unable to hide my sarcasm.

He smiled again and escorted me through the doors, heading towards the concession stand. "Want anything to drink?"

I shook my head. "I'm fine." I was looking all around us. I think I expected to see Tabatha skulking around somewhere, maybe in the shadows watching us to see the progress of their ruse.

By the time we entered the theater that our movie was showing in, I still hadn't been able to locate her. He led me down the aisle towards the middle row, and we both seated ourselves.

Several times during the movie, his arms slid around the back of my seat, just barely touching my shoulders. Once he let his hand fall on my thigh.

Around us, there were several couples making out. I could tell that Zander noticed it too, because he was glancing around just like I was. Maybe he was trying to pick Tabatha out of the crowd, too.

His arm tightened around me and he leaned close to me to whisper, "You look so good tonight, Patty."

I closed my eyes when he said my name. The sound of my name on his lips was too delicious, too tempting. Maybe I could pretend for just a few hours that this was real. Maybe I could pretend for just a few hours that he really liked me and we were really dating. The mind is a powerful thing. I'm sure I could delude myself for just a few hours.

He started nipping at my ear with his teeth and all the while, I could still feel his breath in my ear. I didn't really know how to react. So I didn't. He pulled back and looked down at me. "You don't like me, do you?"

I thought of telling him everything then and there. I thought of letting him have it. I thought of shouting to him that I'd seen him at the mall earlier with Tabatha, that I knew they were still an item, and that I knew that all of this stuff with me was just some sick joke. I thought a lot of things in those few minutes.

I didn't let him have it. I didn't shout and scream at him. I leaned close to him and kissed him. He was shocked at first, but after a moment, he was returning the kiss and raising a hand to caress my hair.

I let myself savor that moment. In that moment, I didn't worry about when he and Tabatha were going to drop the bomb on me. I didn't think about what a lying, deceitful person he was. I just focused on how good it felt to kiss him and have his arms around me.

We both pulled back from the kiss at the same time. He looked down at me and I looked up at him. Neither of us was sure about what was happening in the movie. That was the farthest thing from our minds.

He started to say something, but stopped himself.

No, please tell me, I thought. *Please tell me that you made a mistake in trusting Tabatha. Please tell me that you were planning a joke on me, but that you can't go through with it.* "You...were going to say something," I whispered to him.

He shook his head. "I was just going to tell you what a cool girl you are," he said with his eyes fixed on the movie screen.

My bottom lip trembled, but I turned to look at the movie screen too, even though I didn't know what was going on in the film. I'd lost track of too much of the plot to know what the characters were doing or why.

When the movie was finally over, we both stood and exited the theater. He led the way without holding my hand. He seemed to be deep in thought. Maybe he was regretting getting into this. Maybe he didn't want to play the joke on me anymore.

I simply followed him without speaking, since he didn't seem to be in the mood for talking. We both got in the car. He didn't bother to open the door for me so I opened it for myself. We rode in silence until he reached forward and turned on the radio. Hard rock music blasted from the speakers and made the tiny car shudder with each drum beat.

I leaned forward and turned the volume of the music down. "You're very distant," I said. "What are you thinking about?"

"A lot of things," he said vaguely.

"Like what?" I asked.

He turned and looked at me. "Us."

My heart did flip flops beneath my chest. "What do you mean?"

"I don't even know what I mean. I just-"

"I know about you and Tabatha," I blurted out. Shocked at myself, I covered my mouth with my hands.

He frowned. "What?"

With my eyes wide, I looked at him and dropped my hands into my lap. "I saw both of you. Today, at the mall. You guys looked like a happy couple."

His mouth set into a firm line.

"To be honest, I didn't even expect you to show up tonight."

"After breaking up with me yesterday, she called me and asked me to forgive her," he explained. "She wanted to get back together with me, but I told her no. She asked if we could still be friends and I told her that we could. She asked me out to the mall earlier today. I didn't really want to go, but I figured I did have some things to buy anyway. For our date. So I went."

"You went shopping for our date?" I couldn't help but ask.

He nodded. "This entire outfit is new. And I got you something...but I left it at home. I thought that maybe it was a little too soon to give it to you."

I sat back in my seat, not sure what to think.

"You thought that I was trying to date you and Tabatha at the same time?" he asked me.

"I thought you and Tabatha were playing a cruel joke on me," I confessed. *A part of me still does.*

He had the grace to look surprised. "You think I'd do something like that to you?"

"I don't know what to believe sometimes," I admitted. "You seem like a sweet, great guy, but you've been going out with Tabatha for a long time now. If you're going out with her, then you have to be attracted to her for some reason. And if you're attracted to her, despite what a psychotic monster she is, then something needs to be screwy with you too."

He seemed stunned by my words.

I shrugged unapologetically. "If you're going to play a mean joke on me, you can admit it. It won't hurt my feelings...much."

He pulled the car over and sat quietly for a few minutes. He stared down at his hands, then out of the windshield, and then he finally turned to face me. "Tabatha is a beautiful girl. And she can be charming and witty when she wants to be. She's not always...psychotic, as you put it. Sometimes she's very sweet."

"She hasn't been sweet lately," I muttered. "At least, not to me. I've never had much of a problem with her before, but lately she's been uncontrollable."

"She's under a lot of pressure right now," he said. "She doesn't have the best relationship with her parents and the only friends that she has talk about her behind her back. On top of all of that, she's expected to cheer and smile and lead an entire cheerleading squad that smiles in her face, but hates her guts."

When he put it like that, I guess maybe Tabatha didn't have it as easy as I thought. "So basically, you're saying that pretty girls have problems too."

He chuckled at that. "Everyone has problems, especially high school kids. When you're in high school, it doesn't matter who you are or what you look like. You're going to have issues."

This was the side of Zander that I liked, the side that talked genuinely and wisely. "I guess you're right," I agreed.

"I'm going to be honest. I'm not in the mood to go to a stuffy restaurant right now," he said.

"Neither am I."

"But I don't want the night to end yet."

"Neither do I."

He lifted a hand and tenderly stroked my cheek. "I like you a lot, Patty."

"You barely know anything about me," I couldn't stop myself from saying in amazement. "What could you possibly like about me?"

He laughed. "Your honesty, for one. You say things that a lot of other girls wouldn't dare to say in front of me. You don't walk on eggshells when you're with me. You say whatever you're thinking. And you're adorable."

Adorable? Me?

He leaned towards me and kissed me again. His lips tasted sweet. His breath caressed my lips. He had his hands tangled in my hair and his hands were all over me. Ricky and I hadn't really kissed or made out a lot, so I felt very inexperienced. I didn't know where to put my hands and I didn't know how I should position my body.

He seemed to sense that I was uncomfortable, because he drew back. "There are a lot of things I want to say to you," he said softly.

"Then say them."

"I can't."

"Okay."

He smiled and shook his head. "I'm not as experienced at speaking my mind as you are."

"That's fine," I told him.

"Be patient with me."

"Okay."

He lifted a hand to my cheek again, but this time his hand felt icy cold against my cheek. I flinched away from it. "I should probably get you home," he said, straightening and pulling the car away from the curb.

chapter six

"And *then* what happened?"

"And then he took me home," I said.

A loud squeal sounded on the other end of the line.

I laughed. "Mary, come on," I chided. "Just because we went out on one date doesn't mean anything."

"Rumor has it that he wants to ask you to Homecoming, Patty," Mary said.

I didn't even want to think about it. Homecoming was a big deal in Vista Heights. Some of the girls flew out of town just to buy their dresses. He wouldn't dare ask me to such a high profile dance. He didn't mind being seen in public with me, but he was Zander Davis! He could date anyone he wanted in the entire school.

Still, I fantasized that he *did* take me to Homecoming. And that everyone saw us together and flipped their lids. Because they *would* flip their lids if they saw us show up to the Homecoming Dance together. Everyone would totally lose their minds.

I talked to Mary for a few more minutes, and then I collapsed into bed.

I woke up late the next morning. By the time I stumbled out of my family's house, I'd missed the school bus by about fifteen minutes. There was a sleek, red car parked at the curb of my house. The car looked familiar and it took me a moment to realize that it was Zander's car.

He stepped out of the car and beckoned me over. "Do you want to be late?" He glanced at his watch. "Come on, let's go."

I could barely get my feet to move. Had he really come to pick me up for school? I felt like I was in a dreamland. On the way to school, we passed by the Hidden Treasures store. The store owner was standing in the doorway and seemed to peer inside of the car. An eerie smile stretched across his face and he lifted his hand in a wave.

His words rang in my ears. *"I sell dreams,"* he had said.

Zander pulled up to the school and turned off the car. Instead of getting out of the car, he just kind of sat there. Then he turned to me and asked me, "So you're going to Homecoming with me, right?"

I guess you could say I was floating on air for the rest of the day. He always seemed to have that effect on me. He didn't have to do much to make me feel special. I couldn't believe that out of all of the girls in school, he wanted to go to the Homecoming Dance with me.

My friends were gathered around my locker, probably hoping to see Zander and me together. He gave me a peck on the cheek, greeted my friends, and was off to his first period class.

Dana, Stephanie, and Mary squealed with delight and made a circle around me. They wanted me to tell them "everything," but I didn't have time to go into the story just then. First period was going to start and I told them as much. I wouldn't be able to tell them the story at lunch because they had a different lunch period than I did. They'd have to wait for the end of the day.

I could tell that my friends didn't like the idea of that, but they did agree that we should all hurry to our first period classes before we were late. Still, they clapped me on the back and were giddy with happiness. They may have been even happier than I was.

I walked through the halls in a daze. It seemed that Tabatha wasn't at school that day, because I didn't see her in the gym class that we shared together. That was just another reason why my day seemed to go perfectly. Then there was Ricky.

He showed up at my locker out of nowhere. One minute, I had my locker open. The next, I closed my locker door and there he was, standing right next to me. I almost jumped out of my skin. "Hi, Ricky," I greeted.

"Hi, Patty," he said.

"I haven't seen you in awhile."

"I know. It feels like it's been a really long time."

"How have you been?"

"I've been good," he said with a nod of his head. "But not as good as you. I hear you've been going out with Zander."

"We've been hanging out," I said carefully, not wanting to feed the rumor mills.

"I hear it's a little more serious than that," Ricky said. "I mean, come on. He asked you to Homecoming?"

"Yeah," I said casually. "He did."

"He's bad news, Patty."

I almost laughed in his face. "What do you care? You *dumped* me, or did you forget that?"

He shrugged his shoulders. "I just wanted to warn you. He's bad news. He's up to something."

"Of *course* he's up to something, Ricky!" I shouted. "He's the most popular guy in school and he's going out with the fat girl. Tell me what *isn't* wrong with that picture."

Ricky looked shocked at my words. He looked like he didn't know what to say.

I tossed my hair over one shoulder in the way that Tabatha did sometimes.

"You're talking differently, you're walking differently, and you're dressing differently," Ricky said in a soft voice. "What is that guy turning you into?"

"His girlfriend," I snapped. "Get over it." I turned on my heel and left him standing there.

When my mother found out that I was going to Homecoming with the most popular guy in school, even she wanted a hand in helping me shop for my dress. She let me use her credit card. It's the first time she ever let me use her credit card; I think it's the first time I've ever even *used* a credit card. Of course, she let me know not to get too pricey with the dress and accessories that I chose.

Mary and Stephanie had after-school jobs, so they had to work the Wednesday before Homecoming, but Dana agreed to go shopping with me. The mall wasn't extremely crowded since it was a weeknight, but there were some students that I recognized from school. A couple of them were working in some of the stores.

I peered at some of the dresses on the department store racks. I didn't have the luxury of flying to New York City to pick out a designer dress that no one else would be wearing, like some of the rich girls in my school. But I didn't care. Two hundred girls could be wearing dresses exactly like mine and I'd still be happy, because I would be dancing with the hottest guy I'd ever set my eyes on.

I fell in love with a crimson red dress at one of the department stores. I tried the dress on and it actually fit me perfectly. Dana gave two thumbs up signs, showing me her approval. Thursday and Friday were pretty uneventful. Zander had football practice both days, so we weren't able to hang out. I had homework to do both of those days anyway, and I needed to get caught up in my studies.

The next time I'd see him would actually be on the night of Homecoming, which was Saturday.

Saturday morning I woke up early. I had an appointment to get my hair and nails done. I'd never had my hair or nails professionally styled before. Mary and Stephanie were also going to Homecoming with their dates, so we all went to the same salon and chatted while getting our nails painted.

"Billy is so goofy sometimes," Mary was saying as she blew on her nails. "I don't know how serious I am about him. There are times when I really like spending time with him, but then there are times when I feel he's too childish for me."

"If Dana were here, she'd say that all boys are childish," Stephanie said, laughing.

It was true. Dana wasn't going to Homecoming. She was probably still asleep, even though it was near noon.

"I can't wait to see what your dress looks like, Patty," Stephanie said. "I bet it's gorgeous."

"What color is it?" Mary asked.

"I'm not saying," I told her, and pursed my lips shut to prove my point.

We all brought our dresses to Stephanie's house. Her family has a lot of money and their house is huge. They used to have a maid and a butler, but they no longer did. Supposedly, the maid had been snooping through Mrs. Foster's belongings. Creepy.

The house was still beautiful though, with a long stretch of front yard and a back yard that led into a meadow. The house itself was a brick, two-story manor with large, picture windows and elegant balconies.

If Zander was Ken doll, then Stephanie was Barbie and had the dream house to prove it. We all followed Stephanie into the house and headed up to her room, where we hung our dresses up in her closet.

I was a novice at applying makeup, so while Stephanie applied her own makeup and while Mary applied her own makeup, they both took a turn at applying makeup on me. I squirmed and struggled against them at some points, but the end product was well worth the trouble. I looked in the mirror and I didn't even recognize myself. With the hair, the makeup, and the nails, I had somehow managed to look like a young movie star.

All that was left was the dress, which I hurriedly pulled from the closet. I stepped into the dress and felt like I was stepping into another person. I pulled the strapless dress up.

"Oh my God!" Mary exclaimed. "Patty has cleavage!"

I did. I couldn't help but giggle.

"You look so hot, Patty," Stephanie said in wonderment.

I *felt* hot. I straightened the dress and looked at my reflection again. "You're hot," I told my reflection with a confident smile. "You're really hot."

Mary's spaghetti strap dress was the deepest shade of blue I'd ever seen. Her dark hair was pinned up, leaving her pale shoulders bare. Curly tendrils framed her face and teardrop earrings graced both ears. She admired her reflection in the vanity mirror.

Standing at her back was Stephanie, whose emerald green halter-styled dress was sure to stand out in a crowd. The hem of the dress kissed the tops of her matching heels. Her flaxen gold hair was styled into coiled ringlets that bounced whenever she turned her head this way or that. Tiny studs pierced through both of her ears.

The guys showed up about an hour later, while Stephanie, Mary, and I were running around the house fretting about how good we looked. I'd had to call Zander on his cell phone to let him know that I'd be at Stephanie's house instead of my parent's house.

He showed up to the house last, complete with a bouquet of flowers and a corsage. Aw. Maybe I don't give him enough credit sometimes. I stood on tiptoe and gave him a kiss on his cheek.

His appraisal of me made me feel special and pretty. He grabbed my hand, raised it above my head, and twirled me around like a ballerina. Then he ducked his head down and kissed me shortly after telling me how beautiful I was. I came close to tears, I really did.

"I know you guys said you didn't have enough money to get a limo after all of the shopping you did," he said seriously, addressing us all. "And I know you said that it

didn't matter to you whether or not you had a limo, but..."
He swung the front door open so that we could all clearly see
a sleek, black stretch limo parked in the Fosters' driveway.

Mary and Stephanie squealed. Their dates slapped each
other high-fives. And Zander snaked his arm around my
waist. We filed through the front door after my friends.

I climbed into the limousine and sat next to Zander. I sat
as closely to him as humanly possible without *becoming*
him.

We were loud and obnoxious, but we were teenagers
and we were having fun. We joked around with each other
and chatted until the limousine parked in front of our high
school, where other vehicles were lined up at the curb.

Zander helped everyone out of the car like the
gentleman that he was. Then he escorted me inside. He
handed the student body president our tickets and we stepped
into the gymnasium, which had been decorated with a
fairytale theme. *How appropriate,* I thought to myself as
Zander immediately dragged me onto the dance floor.

Stephanie and Mary and their dates danced alongside us.
We gained the attention of most of the student body as we
danced and goofed.

The music and the atmosphere were upbeat. Everyone
seemed to be enjoying themselves. Zander held me close to
him and I danced with my head pressed to his chest.

A disco ball was attached to the ceiling, and it twirled
and cast sparkles and light on the floor and on all of the
students. It was like a scene out of a daydream, or straight
out of a fairytale.

The music paused and the deejay spoke into the
microphone. "All of the votes are in for the Homecoming
King and Queen! May I please introduce the principal, Mr.
Carlson, who will announce the winners!"

All of the students stopped dancing and clapped where
they stood.

Mr. Carlson, who looked way too young to be a
principal, walked onto the stage with a white envelope in his

hands. He waved at the crowd. Most of the female students had a crush on him. With his dark hair, light eyes, and toned build, he was quite attractive.

He stood at the microphone and looked over the crowd. "Are you all having a good time?" he asked the audience.

Everyone shouted and screamed at the top of their lungs.

"I don't think I heard you," he bellowed into the microphone. "Are you having a good time?" He shot a hand into the air, the hand holding the white envelope. In that exact moment, he looked like a rock star.

The crowd went nuts as if he *was* a rock star.

I laughed and leaned against Zander. His left hand closed around my right hand.

"What I have here are the results for the Homecoming King and Queen," Mr. Carlson said, waving the envelope in front of his face. "Are you as ready as I am to find out who the winners are?"

The crowd lost their minds again.

The principal chuckled into the microphone and gestured for everyone to settle down. "All right, all right. First up, we have the Homecoming King, right?" He tore open the envelope, read the text on the card, and shouted into the mike, "As if it's any surprise! Zander, get up here!"

Zander squeezed my hand and surged through the crowd, giving a high-five to a couple of his friends along the way. Instead of using the stairs to get to the stage, he walked to the front of the stage and jumped up.

I covered my mouth in surprise.

Mary clapped a hand on my shoulder. "Your boyfriend is crazy!" she shouted.

My boyfriend, I mused to myself happily, watching him climb onstage with Mr. Carlson.

He bowed his head and allowed Mr. Carlson to crown him. Mr. Carlson didn't hesitate before shouting into the microphone, "We've got to have a Homecoming Queen! I mean, there's no Homecoming King without his Queen, right?" He paused to look down at the card in his hands.

My palms were sweating. Was he about to announce Tabatha's name? Was she here somewhere, watching Zander and I with evil eyes, waiting to spring some nasty trick on us?

Mr. Carlson shouted into the microphone, "Patty Coben, get up here!"

The audience got quiet. The silence was deafening. I didn't even think I had heard Mr. Carlson right. He couldn't have said my name. Could he have?

Mary's eyes were wide as she turned to look at me. Stephanie also looked shocked. The three of us must have looked like crazy people.

"Patty? Patty Coben, you out there?" Mr. Carlson shaded a hand over his eyes to block out the blinding lights.

I stumbled forward and the crowd parted for me. Everyone was looking at me and whispering to the person beside them. I'm sure they were all asking, "Did *you* vote for her?"

My mouth was dry. My eyes were watery. My mind was racing. By the time I got up to the stage, I was a wreck. I was sure I couldn't speak if I'd been asked to.

Mr. Carlson set a crown on top of my head and gave me a charming smile. "Congratulations, Patty," he said, and stepped back. "Congratulate your new Homecoming King and Queen!"

The audience paused before losing their minds this time. It seemed that they no longer cared about who voted for me or how I'd gotten voted Homecoming Queen. They were here to let loose and have fun, and they would do just that.

Zander collected me in his arms and held me close to him, leaning down to plant a kiss on my lips. The audience screamed even louder.

"What an adorable couple," came a voice over the speakers strategically positioned throughout the gymnasium.

I didn't know where the voice was coming from, but I recognized the voice. I think Zander did too, because his grip on me tightened.

Tabatha appeared on the stage with a microphone in her hand.

chapter seven

Tabatha smiled a dangerous smile and spoke into the microphone again. "You guys are so cute together, really," she said. "If I had my camera phone with me, I'd snap a picture of you two and make it my screensaver. You look so darling."

Someone in the audience offered their camera phone to Tabatha.

She tossed her hair over one shoulder. "And you, Patty, *especially*. You look downright *hot* in that dress. I would have never thought it possible."

Even though I knew that a catty remark would follow the compliment, I couldn't help but feel flattered. After all, the compliment was coming from Tabatha Andrews.

She approached Zander and me, fatally attractive in a black satin sheath of a dress that her body must have been poured into. It clung to her like a second skin. Her hair had been styled in a regal updo and her eyelids had been darkened with eyeshadow. "You look adorable, you really do, Patty. It's a shame that Zander can't stand the sight of you."

I rolled my eyes at her, but I was sweating bullets. What was she talking about?

"At first I thought our plan was in jeopardy," Tabatha continued, as if talking to herself. "I mean, he told me how you saw both of us in the mall. And I thought, for sure you'd figured us out. We wouldn't be able to fool you after that. But lo and behold Zander, the wonderful actor he is, managed to string you along still." She grabbed his jaw in her hand and smiled lovingly at him.

The audience was confused and so was I, but I kept my mouth shut until I had the full picture.

"The school was fooled, too, it looks like," Tabatha said, finally acknowledging the audience. "I can't believe *they* didn't suspect anything. Zander is the quarterback for our football team, and *you*? You're a *nobody*. And a fat nobody at that. How could he ever grow to like you?"

I turned to Zander and even though I willed the tears away, I could feel them collecting at the corners of my eyes. "She's lying, right?"

He looked down at me. There was a battle going on behind his eyes. He opened his mouth to speak, but Tabatha didn't give him the opportunity.

"No, I'm not *lying*," she spat at me. "Why would I have to lie about anything? *Look* at me."

I tore my eyes away from Zander and did as she demanded.

"I'm beautiful," she continued, circling around Zander and I. "I'm downright *gorgeous*. All of the boys at this school want me, and all of the girls in this school want to *be* me. Who would want to be you? No one. If I looked like you, I'd kill myself. You're not *pretty*. I mean, somehow you managed to look hot tonight, but that's because you're wearing tons of makeup and a dress that costs more than your entire wardrobe did."

The tears spilled down my cheeks. I was mumbling something, but I didn't even know what I was saying, so I doubt she did.

She laughed at me. Once she started laughing, some of the students in the crowd caught on and they started laughing, too. It was all a joke, all one big joke.

She held a hand out to Zander and he gave me one long look before accepting the hand and going to stand beside her. They were both looking at me, staring at me. She laughed at me, but he didn't. I know a part of him cared for me, but it wasn't a big enough part for him to grab the microphone from her and defend me. He did no such thing. He just stood there with his head bowed while she and the rest of our classmates laughed at me.

And I saw red. Everything was tinted in red. I think I may have even been hyperventilating. My breaths were quick and shallow. My fists clenched and unclenched rapidly. I felt dizzy and overwhelmed. And then I was falling. *God, don't let me collapse while I'm in my dress. Don't let me fall in front of almost everyone I know. Please, don't.*

But He did. And I fell flat on my back. I could still hear them laughing, and then Tabatha blocked out all of the light as she stood over me and looked down at me.

That's when I blacked out.

I didn't understand the concept of embracing my rage until that night. The day that I'd seen Tabatha and Zander together in the mall, I thought I'd embraced my rage then. But I hadn't...not until the night of the Homecoming Dance. That night, I changed. I walked into the Homecoming Dance as Patty Coben and I walked out of that school building as...someone else, someone I couldn't recognize.

Over the next few days, my friends tried calling me and visiting me. I gave my family strict orders to tell everyone that I couldn't talk on the phone or wasn't at home. I didn't show up to school Monday.

I pulled out the pamphlet that I'd gotten from Hidden Treasures. I studied it, flipped it over in my hands. There was more text on page three; I knew it without looking. I'd embraced my rage. Now there was another step waiting for me.

I finally got tired of waiting and flipped the book open to the third page.

Step 3: bind her hair with yours

I propped the book open with one of my shoes and plucked out a strand of my own hair. Tucked within some of the last pages of the pamphlet were the strands of dark hair belonging to Tabatha. I twisted the strand of my hair to hers, and as I sat there, the letters formed on the fourth page.

Step 4: light a black candle

I didn't own a black candle, which meant that I had to pay another visit to my new favorite store owner. I had to pay a visit to Aidan Powers at Hidden Treasures.

Aidan wasn't standing in the doorway of his shop as he usually was when I saw him. He was at the cash register ringing up some merchandise for a customer. I waited until he was done with the customer before approaching him.

He didn't look surprised to see me. "How is the pamphlet working out for you?" he asked me casually.

"It's working well," I replied.

He smiled. "You came for help." It wasn't a question; it was a statement.

I nodded. "I need a black candle."

He crossed his arms over his chest. "Step 4."

"Yes."

"Follow me."

I did. I followed him to an aisle filled with nothing but candles, of every size, shape, and color. He pulled a large, black candle off of the shelf and led me to the register.

"That will be four hundred dollars," he told me.

My eyes must have bulged out of my head.

He grinned. "I'm just kidding. You can have this candle free of charge."

I cocked my head to the side. "How do you make any money?" I asked him.

"It's something that I often wonder to myself," he said, wrapping up my candle and sliding it into an ordinary brown paper bag.

I took the candle home with me, and with the book open to the fifth page, I lit it. The letters slowly appeared on the page as if they had been there all along. They told me to chant a certain arrangement of words, which I did, over and over again. I chanted until more letters appeared on page six.

Step 6: sleep

Sleep? How am I supposed to do that? I wondered this and still, I climbed into bed and turned off the lamp on my nightstand. There were a dozen questions that I had. What was this pamphlet going to do for me? What would welcome me when I opened my eyes? Why was it telling me what to do? Why did it want me to bind my hair with Tabatha's?

There was a nightmare waiting for me when I lost consciousness.

I was running through the woods. I didn't recognize the area, but I was either chasing someone or I was being chased. I had the impression that I was chasing someone, because I never looked over my shoulder.

There was a trail of a nightgown up ahead of me. I ran as quickly as I could, trying to catch up to whoever was ahead of me.

I was filled with so much rage. I wanted to kill the person that I was chasing. I wanted to close my hands around her throat until the life flickered from her eyes.

Hidden Treasures: Switched

I was finally gaining on her. She looked like she couldn't keep up the pace much longer. She slowed down. She stopped running altogether and was panting hard. I caught up to her and wheeled her around. And I was looking into my own face.

chapter eight

I sat up straight in bed and rubbed the sleep from my eyes. I stretched and yawned. *What a horrible nightmare,* I thought to myself. *Why would I dream about chasing myself? It doesn't make much sense.*

I opened my eyes and looked around my room...except I wasn't looking around my room. My bedroom window wasn't to the right of my bed; it was to the left of my bed. And since when had my bed grown a canopy over it? The colors were totally wrong. The setting of the furniture was off, and the furniture itself wasn't familiar. The bedroom that I was in had a fairy princess theme to it, and I wasn't nine years old. I was seventeen.

I tossed the pink comforter aside, mentally noting that *my* comforter had a floral print on it. Then, I jumped out of bed and opened the door to my room. I was greeted with a hallway I didn't recognize. While the bedroom had a fairy princess theme, the hallway was lined with cedar walls and decorated with a narrow table. On top of the table there was a slender vase filled beyond the brim with dark-colored flowers.

Uncertainly, I stepped out of the bedroom. Was I still dreaming? Was it possible that I had dreamed about waking up, when I was still, in fact, asleep?

I guess it could be possible. It had to be *more* than possible. It had to be *probable,* because I was walking around a house that was unfamiliar to me. I headed down the hallway and found a staircase. I didn't think twice before plummeting down the stairs at full speed, hoping to find my family in our kitchen.

What I found in the kitchen was definitely a family, but it wasn't mine. There was a slim, grouchy looking man with short, dark hair, a hawkish nose, and brown eyes shielded by a stylish pair of eyeglasses. He was seated at the kitchen table scowling at the newspaper.

There was a dark-haired woman standing in front of the refrigerator. She was humming. I didn't recognize the tune that she was humming and I'm not sure I wanted to.

"Where are my parents?" I demanded to know.

Both the man and the woman directed their attention to me. The woman rolled her eyes dramatically and closed the refrigerator door after finding what she was looking for. She carried an oversized bowl to the kitchen counter. "After all, we couldn't possibly be your parents," she said with a hint of sarcasm in her voice.

I frowned and looked in the direction of the man. "What am I doing here? This isn't my house."

"Before the antics, could you please sit down to breakfast?" the man said over the top of his newspaper. "I don't want you to be late for school."

School? How could anyone think of school? And didn't they find it odd that I was some strange girl who'd walked into their kitchen? A thought occurred to me. I voiced it out loud without really meaning to. "Have I been kidnapped?"

The woman shook her head as she turned on the stove. "I think she has lost her mind, Derek."

The man closed the newspaper, took a sip from a steaming mug of coffee, and stood from the table. He walked over to me and looked me over. "You don't *look* like you have a fever," he murmured.

I groaned with exasperation and turned on my heel, exiting the room the same way I'd come in. Behind me I could hear the man and woman talking.

The man muttered, "She's so overdramatic. She must get it from you."

"I don't know *where* she gets it from. It's definitely not me," the woman returned.

I headed back up the stairs. My mind was running several miles per minute. I couldn't even keep up with all of the thoughts jumbling around in my head. This house wasn't my family's house. Those people downstairs weren't my parents. And where was my little brother?

I'd just begun to panic when I passed a floor-length mirror hung on the wall of the upstairs hallway. I saw a flash of dark hair as I walked past the mirror. I halted and retraced my steps, until I ended up in front of the mirror.

The image that greeted me was enough to make me scream. The girl in the mirror wasn't Patty Coben. The girl staring back at me, with the dark brown hair, tanned complexion, and cat-like eyes, was Tabatha Andrews.

part two
tabatha

chapter nine

It takes me forever to wake up. I don't know why. Someone once told me that I'm a night person. I guess you could call me that. I like to stay up late and I hate waking up early. Wednesday morning was just one of those mornings. It took me forever to finally drag myself out of bed.

I had a lot on the agenda for the day. I was supposed to meet with the rest of the cheerleaders before school to discuss our strategy at the state competition. A couple of girls had ideas on moves they wanted to include in our routine.

They're always trying to participate in the choreography of our cheers. I guess they just don't understand the concept of having a cheerleading captain. The cheerleading captain is the one who comes up with all of the moves. If I wanted their help, I'd have no trouble asking for it. But I don't need their help, you see, because I plan on being a famous dance choreographer one day. I plan on being the person that pop stars come to when they need help with their dance moves. Something that can help me get to that level is having my cheer choreography recognized by different talent agents who attend our games and the state cheerleading championships.

If our cheer routine for the state championships was a group effort, then I wouldn't stand out from the crowd. They wouldn't recognize my work for what it is: spectacular. I would fade into the background, with the rest of the doofuses on my cheer squad who will probably end up working in dead-end jobs and marrying deadbeats who weren't worth a fraction of their time.

Do I sound completely horrid? Do I sound mean and cold? Zander says I'm cold sometimes, but I can't help it. I have to look out for myself. No one else will.

And anyway, I'm totally getting off of the subject here. The subject was Wednesday morning. I had a lot of things to do that day, you know? There was the meeting with the cheerleaders in the morning, and then I was supposed to meet Zander at my locker. He's always waiting there for me like a devoted puppy dog. In many ways, he's a lot like a puppy dog. He's always begging for my attention. It doesn't matter how mean I am to him. The next day, he'll be right there at my locker, waiting for me. It's almost pathetic. Almost.

Like with that prank that I wanted to play on Patty Coben. Oh my God, right? Zander usually wouldn't do something like that to someone. He is way too kind to do something like that to somebody. *Usually*. But he still went along with it, because of me. Because I asked him to. That's the kind of guy that Zander is. He's sweet. I even suspect he feels bad for what we did to poor Patty.

Well, that's too bad. Patty was asking for it by embarrassing me in gym class like that. No one talks to me like that. And I never forget when someone has made me feel like an idiot. Never. So I had to get her back, and I knew *just* the way to do it.

Do I feel like a wretched person for what we did to her? Maybe a little bit. I mean, I know I took it way over the top by showing up on the stage like that. From the look on her face, it took her a long time to understand what was even going on. And when she fainted, I thought I was just going to *die*. My plan couldn't have been any more perfect.

That was, of course, until Wednesday morning. It took a long time for me to wake up. I think I'd had a nightmare the night before, but I never do remember my dreams.

When I did wake up, though, I didn't even *feel* right. I don't know how to describe how I felt. I didn't feel sick. I didn't feel nauseous. I didn't feel depressed or sad. I just felt *different*. I didn't feel like myself. The first thing that I do every morning is look in the mirror, but I couldn't even do that. Because the first thing I noticed when I opened my eyes-*besides* how different I felt-is that the room I was in wasn't my own.

I would recognize my room anywhere. It's cute, decorated with pink and white unicorns. I have the most adorable canopy bed and white furniture. Whenever my friends come over, they think I'm crazy. After all, I'm a high school senior about to graduate, and I have the room that should belong to a seven year old. I know. But I love my room. That's all that matters.

So after realizing that I wasn't in my room, naturally I freaked out. Who wouldn't freak out if they woke up in a strange room that wasn't theirs? I jumped out of bed and stared down at the grotesque floral print comforter. Ew. My mother would never buy that. Like...*ever*.

Trembling, I went to stand in front of the mirror on the warped vanity in the corner of the room. Even the vanity could have used a little sprucing up. There was paint peeling off of it and everything. The room was a horror. At least, I thought the room was a disaster until I looked in the mirror and discovered the *true* horror. I found myself staring at a face that wasn't mine.

I lost my mind. I screamed, picked up things from the floor and hurled them at the mirror, and backed up until I tripped over my own bed. Well...that is, I tripped over the bed that wasn't even mine.

I fell flat on my face. I didn't bother to get up. I realized that I must be dreaming. I *certainly* had to be dreaming, because I wasn't Patty Coben. I was Tabatha Andrews, the most popular girl at Vista Heights High. I was Zander's girlfriend. I was the captain of the varsity cheerleading squad, for crying out loud!

I brought myself off of the floor with the realization that I must dreaming. I pulled quite a number on Patty at the Homecoming Dance. Maybe this was my conscious getting back at me for what I did to her. I could understand that. I mean, I *had* been horrid.

With that in mind, I couldn't possibly go to school looking like this, could I? I mean…in Patty's body? Granted, this is just a dream, but what good could it do for me to show up in my dreamland school *as* Patty Coben?

I drew open the closet door and shook my head in disapproval. Her wardrobe was just as tacky as her bedroom. "And she wonders why she's not popular," I couldn't help but grumble out loud. My voice wasn't mine, either, of course. It was Patty's. It was disturbing. I made a conscious decision to speak as rarely as possible.

The door to the room was flung open and a little boy with short blonde hair stood in the doorway. "Mom says it's time for breakfast!" he screamed at the top of his lungs.

I covered my ears with my hands. "Do you have to yell like that?" I demanded.

"Did it annoy you?" he asked.

"Yes," I answered.

He grinned. "Then of course I have to yell like that," he told me. "Hurry up. You're going to be late to school."

"I'm not *going* to school," I told him, folding my arms across my chest.

He poked his head out of the room and shouted down the hall at an earsplitting decibel level, "Moooooom! Patty says she's not going to school!"

I heard a feminine voice, much fainter, call back, "Patty, you *are* going to school!"

I rolled my eyes. Great. That meant showering and dressing in Patty Coben's body. I didn't want to see Patty Coben's body, but I refused to go to school smelling gross. So I took a shower. I barely *fit* in the shower, but I took one. Then when I tried on some of the shirts that didn't look *so* horrible, I found out that half the wardrobe didn't even fit me.

"I can't do this!" I shouted at the ceiling.

The ceiling didn't reply.

I continued dressing, slung my backpack over my shoulder, and headed out of the room. It took me a few minutes to figure out which direction I should be heading, but I finally found the staircase and jogged down the steps carefully. "Where is my car?" I shouted, to no one in particular.

The little monster of a boy ran in front of me. "Your car is wherever my speedboat is," he said, pointing to his head. "In our dreams."

"You've got to be kidding me," I said, shocked. "I don't even drive a car?"

The young boy tilted his head to the side. I didn't think the little snot could muster up an emotion like concern, but he managed to do so. "Are you okay?"

"I'm fine," I snapped. "When are we going to get a ride to school?"

"Mom and Dad never give us rides to school," the boy replied. "It would make them late for work."

"You couldn't mean..." I said, without being able to finish the sentence.

"*Duh*," the boy said, turning his back to me. "We ride the bus."

I could have died. Right then and there, I could have just fallen on the floor and died. How lame could Patty's life really be? I mean, did she really have to ride the bus? I knew she wasn't a senior; she was a junior. I'd started driving at the end of my sophomore year, though.

The day didn't get any better. I managed to catch the bus in time-*barely*. Some of the kids were obnoxious. They called me "Fatty Patty" a couple of times and many of them were talking about what had happened at Homecoming. Of course, no one on this bus had personally gone to the Homecoming Dance. The rumor mill had finally trickled down to them and they were finally catching word about what had happened. It kind of made me proud to hear the kids talking about the Homecoming Dance. After a moment's thought, I had to remind myself that none of this was real. This entire experience was a figment of my imagination, so there was nothing for me to be proud about.

The bus pulled up next to the curb in front of our school. I wasn't seriously going to go through with it. I wasn't seriously going to walk in there as Patty Coben, was I?

I figured I didn't have anything to lose. I mean, as realistic as this dream was, it couldn't be reality. Because in reality, I was Tabatha Andrews and *Patty Coben* was Patty Coben. Since it was a dream, I had to let it play out. So I got off of that bus. And I walked into our school with my backpack slung over my shoulder. I didn't know where Patty's locker was. I had a general idea of where it was, because I'd seen her at it a couple of times…but I didn't know which locker number was hers.

So instead of stopping by her locker, I decided to stop by mine. I was supposed to meet with my fellow cheerleaders, but since this was a dream, I didn't have to worry about that. Even if I did have to worry about that, I was way too late to meet with them now. And if I *did* meet with them, it would be in Patty Coben's body. So I just stopped by my locker. Sure enough, Zander was standing there glancing at his watch every few seconds and craning his neck as he looked for me.

I couldn't help but smile. He was such a great boyfriend. I really didn't show my appreciation for him enough. When he talked about our future together, I usually brushed him off and changed the subject, because I'm too young to be thinking about my future with any boy. But I guess I could see a future with Zander.

I don't know what I planned on doing. I definitely couldn't walk up to him and greet him. He'd think that I was Patty. So I started to turn around, until I heard whistles sounding in the hall. The whistles started near the school entrance. Then they seemed to bounce off of the walls and the floor. My curiosity got the better of me. I'm used to the boys whistling at *me*. Who could they have been whistling at?

I turned around, and it seemed that I was turning around in slow motion. Zander lifted his head too, with an expectant smile on his face. He was used to the whistles that I got whenever I walked into a room. He probably thought that the whistles were for me. Boy, would he be wrong.

At first, I couldn't see who the girl was. I could only see the shape of her, because the sunlight was at her back. I couldn't make out her features. Then, as the school entrance doors swung shut, her features became clearer. The long, dark hair was familiar and so was the outfit that she was wearing. The tight, pink blouse was something I'd bought on sale a few weeks ago at the mall and the short skirt was something that I'd had for nearly six months now. The first time I'd worn that skirt, my first period teacher had tried to throw me out of her classroom. She'd sent me to the principal's office because the skirt was too short.

I'd gone to the principal's office, but not before tugging my shirt down and tugging my skirt down so that my skirt appeared to be knee-length. He'd sent me back to class with a note for Mrs. Foreman. The color had drained from her face. It had been kind of funny.

Nothing was funny about looking at myself dressed in my cute clothes and with my sleek, shiny hair carefully styled. It was…it was *me*, but it couldn't be. Because I was Patty Coben.

The logical part of me had to ask, *If you're Patty Coben, then who is Patty Coben?* Logically, she would be me, right? I mean, it would only make sense.

The girl was looking directly at me with her mouth tugged up at the corner. She winked at me; then she turned her attention to Zander. She whispered something in his ear that made him turn red. *What is she telling him?* I wondered, wishing I was closer so I could hear what she was saying. I was wishing in vain.

She linked her arm with Zander's and they walked together. She hadn't even bothered with my locker. She probably didn't know the locker combination.

I was furious. I was livid. I don't know why. This was just a dream, right? Eventually, I'd wake up and this would all be a figment of my imagination, my just desserts for eating Cherry Garcia ice cream past eleven o' clock at night. But there was something pulling at the back of my mind, some higher awareness that seemed to have implanted itself into my brain. And the higher awareness was whispering to me, *But this isn't a dream. This is real.*

chapter ten

As the day went on, I started to believe that this wasn't a dream. I couldn't come up with a logical explanation for it, but somehow Patty Coben and I had switched bodies. The more I started to suspect that this was real, the more frightened I became. I couldn't go up to my friends and plead my case to them. They'd think I was a nut. Or even worse, they'd think I was Patty Coben and throw their drinks in my face.

I couldn't go to my parents, because they wouldn't know I was me. I definitely couldn't go to Zander. As long as he had a pretty girl on his arm, he'd probably be content with the situation. And of course I don't mean that, because Zander is a really sweet guy. I just didn't know what to do. The only person that I could approach was the enemy. She was the only other person that could have an idea of what was going on.

I approached her during what was supposed to be my lunch break. I expected to see her with a large crowd around her. That's how it always was with me. There was always a large group of people that seemed to appear around me during lunch. Sometimes it was girls wanting to know what they could do to look like me, sometimes it was some of the cheerleaders trying to plan a get-together or a shopping spree, and sometimes it was a group of guys telling me that they could be a much better boyfriend than Zander was.

Surprisingly enough, she was sitting by herself in the cafeteria. She had an intense look on her face, as if she were in deep thought. I dropped my lunch tray on the table in front of her.

Her eyes slowly lifted to meet mine. We didn't exchange words for a long time. We just stood there looking at each other. She surveyed the hideous baggy jeans and plain white t-shirt that I was wearing. Whereas she looked like she was trying not to laugh, looking at her nearly took my breath away.

"How did you do this?" I asked her.

"How did I do what?" she asked casually, picking an apple up from my tray and biting into it.

I was seething with anger. "You know exactly what I'm talking about."

"I have no clue as to what you're talking about," she insisted. She took another bite of the apple. *Crunch.*

"You stole my body," I accused through clenched teeth. "And I want it back."

"I stole your *body*?" she repeated. "Have you finally lost it, Coben?"

"My name isn't Coben," I whispered savagely. "My name is Tabatha Andrews, and-"

"What is going on here?" Zander interrupted smoothly, approaching the table. He never ate the junk that our cafeteria served. He always sneaked out into the parking lot, drove down the street to the burger joint, and brought his lunch back with him to the cafeteria. He looked me up and down, dropping his greasy fast food bag onto the cafeteria table. "Hi, Patty."

My gut wrenched when he called me that. And the way he was looking at me gave me the creeps. He was looking at me like he *pitied* me.

He ran a hand through his hair and said sheepishly, "I kind of wanted to apologize for the Homecoming Dance. I didn't know it would get that out of hand. I thought it was just a simple joke."

I watched the other girl's eyes as he spoke the words. Anger flashed there, but she quickly blinked it away and lifted her eyes back up to me. "Yeah, we're both *really* sorry," she said with a sugary sweet smile on her face. "I probably got a little too carried away. I can't imagine how embarrassing it was for you."

"It really wasn't that embarrassing at all," I said, finally finding my voice. "Later on that night, I actually laughed about it."

Zander looked impressed. "Really?"

I shrugged my shoulders. "Yeah. I mean, what are you going to do, right?"

The other girl shrugged her shoulders, losing interest in the entire conversation.

Zander clapped me on the back. "You're a real sport, Patty."

I backed away from them, nodding like an idiot. I didn't know what else to do. There she was, sharing lunch with *my* boyfriend...and what was she doing? Was she snacking on French fries? Was she taking the wrapper off of a cheeseburger? I *never* ate cheeseburgers or fries. They were stuffed with fattening calories. Not that I didn't crave a cheeseburger or fries once in awhile. I often did, but I had good self-control.

Look where my good self-control got me, I thought to myself, watching in disgust as my body was being ruined by a greasy fast food cheeseburger.

I walked away from that table, but I didn't walk away without a goal. I didn't know how, but I was going to get my body back.

I don't know where I came up with the idea of stalking the *real* Patty. I just know that I didn't feel comfortable in her family's house with her annoying little brother and her bland parents. Her friends tried contacting me a few times, but I didn't have a desire to talk to them. They couldn't offer any help to me, not with the situation that I was dealing with.

Since I didn't feel comfortable in Patty Coben's surroundings, I decided that I could learn more about the real Patty by stalking her. There are several flaws in my plan, however. The first problem that comes to mind is the fact that I had no car. Patty was no doubt riding around in my pink Miata now, so she probably had a set of wheels at her beck and call, while I was left high and dry.

On Friday night, I started writing down plans. It might be possible to solve my vehicle issues by responding to the phone calls that I was getting from Patty's friends. Maybe one of them drove a car.

It was while I was making these plans that one of my closest friends-and rivals-was being brutally murdered.

chapter eleven

"Oh my God, did you hear what happened?" Mary Blume asked with wide, green eyes.

Mary and Dana Myers both showed up on the doorstep of the Coben household nearly an hour before we were due in school on Monday morning. I'd still been asleep, but Mrs. Coben came to wake me up since my "friends" were on the doorstep.

I shook my head in response to Mary's question. "What happened?"

"Shelly Woods was killed last night," Dana responded, leaning against the doorjamb with her arms folded across her chest.

I couldn't hide my shock. "What?"

Mary nodded emphatically. Her dark hair was pulled into a short ponytail. She gestured wildly with her hands whenever she talked. I'd noticed her in the halls before, but I'd never paid much attention to her. Usually, she was really quiet. Now, she couldn't seem to shut up. "A janitor found her in the locker room shower last night. They're saying that her head was smashed in."

Dana wrinkled her nose in disgust. "From what people are saying, the blood was everywhere. They're not even letting us inside the school. Classes have been called off until further notice."

"There are police cars all over the place," Mary chimed in.

Shelly had been murdered at our school? Who could have done such a thing? I shuddered at the thought of attending school with someone cold and calculating enough to do something like that.

I invited Dana and Mary inside for breakfast. They entered the house behind me. I figured that since they'd stopped by, I might as well put my plan into motion. "I came up with this really great idea," I announced as I led them into the kitchen. I still hadn't really learned my way around the kitchen, but I blindly opened and closed several cabinets before I found bowls and utensils.

"What idea?" Dana asked, seating herself at the table.

"After what happened at the Homecoming Dance...well, naturally, I want some kind of retaliation."

Mary's eyes nearly bugged out of her head. "Against Tabatha?" she asked in a tiny voice.

I nodded my head. "Yes."

"After what happened to Shelly, I'm not sure *now* is the best time to retaliate," Dana said.

"I don't mean anything drastic," I hurried to say. "I just want to follow her around for awhile. Get some dirt on her. You know...embarrass her the way she did me."

Dana seemed to think it over. "There's bound to be a lot of dirt we can find on her," she said, thinking out loud. "It shouldn't take us too long to come up with something major enough to embarrass her. She probably wears a retainer to sleep or something."

Trying not to take personal offense to the comment, I managed a weak smile. "Yeah. Something like that."

Mary shrugged her shoulders.

Dana rolled her eyes. "I guess we can use my car."

Resisting the urge to do cartwheels across the kitchen floor, I steadily poured myself a bowl of bran cereal. I finally had a stakeout car.

I should have felt more sadness over what had happened to Shelly, but there were times when I felt like I could have snapped her neck myself. She was always saying idiotic things at the wrong times, and always had an opinion about something. I don't think she had a clue as to what *tact* was or how to use it effectively. She was always running off at the mouth about this, that, or the other, and always getting on someone's bad side. You could even say that I wasn't surprised that she got on the wrong person's bad side. It was almost inevitable.

And I really hate to say this because it makes me sound shallow, but my main concern was getting my body back. It was a tragedy, what happened to Shelly, especially being killed so brutally, but she kind of had it coming to her.

Whereas *me*, I'm just an innocent bystander who had her body stolen by some psychotic, chubby outcast who didn't have a life to call her own.

Granted, it wasn't so bad living the life of the psychotic, chubby outcast. I never would have thought I'd say such a thing, but it's true. I mean, since I'm chubby already, I can eat as many carbohydrates as I want. I can eat as much candy as I want and not worry about putting on weight. I don't have to keep up with the rigorous cheerleading schedule. Of course, if I didn't get my body back, I'd probably never be a famous dance choreographer, but I try to focus on the positive. On the positive side, I didn't have to maintain the high profile life of Tabatha Andrews. I didn't have to be a people pleaser and work so hard at impressing everyone. I could just relax and enjoy the simple life.

And Patty's friends were sweet and fun, even though they didn't know a thing about fashion. On the rare moments when I wasn't obsessing about getting my body back, I was actually having fun with them.

I do hate to say this, but because of Shelly's untimely death and due to the school closing, this week was the perfect week to start our stakeout.

Dana drove a small blue Dodge Neon. I rode in the front seat. Mary and Stephanie were in the backseat arguing over which movie star was hotter, Steven Strait or Josh Hartnett.

Dana was fussing with the radio station as she drove. I sat in the passenger seat, staring out of the window.

Someone in my life should have realized that I wasn't being myself lately. Patty didn't walk like me or talk like me. She was probably wasting her time doing *homework*. She probably didn't know that as long as you were captain of the cheerleading squad and as long as the cheerleading squad won state competitions, doing homework wasn't even necessary. She'd probably caused my body to gain five pounds by now.

And what about Zander? How come *he* hadn't realized that there was something different about me? He was supposed to know me inside and out. Surely he had to suspect *something*.

Dana came to park in front of the Andrews household, my family's house. It was so early in the morning that she hadn't changed out of her sky blue fleece pajamas. On this early Wednesday morning, school was still out until further notice.

Stephanie broke out a magazine while we were waiting. She looked nearly as comfortable as Dana did, in a gray hoodie and matching sweatpants. Her blonde hair was piled on top of her head in a sloppy topknot.

"We should have probably started the stakeout later tonight," Dana muttered after half an hour passed. "Not much is going on."

"She could be *anywhere* later on tonight," I told her. "We have to catch her when we can and follow her for the entire day."

"I don't have that much gas in my car," Dana said uncertainly, checking out her gas gauge.

I rolled my eyes. "I'll chip in some gas money."

Dana laughed. "Since when do you have money?"

The real me has money, I thought to myself, feeling a twinge of homesickness.

"This model is way too thin," Stephanie was saying. She was seated directly behind me, flipping through a magazine. "She should really eat something."

Mary, who'd been text messaging her boyfriend on her cell phone, peered at the magazine. "Who could possibly think she looks good?"

"Let me see," I said, and Stephanie handed the magazine to me. "Oh, her. You don't think she's beautiful? I always wished that I could get my waist to be that tiny. And see how little her arms are? I always thought mine were too big."

The car had grown really quiet.

I looked up from the magazine to find everyone staring at me. "What?" I demanded defensively.

"You can't be serious about thinking she's beautiful," Dana said, snatching the magazine away from me and nearly ripping it in half in the process. "She's a *twig*. She's a stick. If she turned to the side, she would disappear. She's that skinny."

"She's not *that* skinny," I argued. "She's…slim."

"*Slim?*" Dana asked incredulously. "You're delusional."

I shrugged my shoulders.

Stephanie spoke up from behind me. "And since when do you wish your waist was skinny?"

"You've never told me you thought your arms were too big," Mary said.

I shrugged again. I really had to remember whose body I was in before I went blabbing my true opinions about things. "There's always room for self-improvement, right?"

"Making yourself look like Skeletor isn't considered improving yourself," Dana quipped.

"Wait a minute…I think that's her," I said, glad to have a diversion. I recognized my pink Miata pulling out of the driveway.

Dana started the car and followed the Miata. "Where is she going this early?"

"Don't stay too close behind her," I warned. "You don't want her to suspect she's being followed."

"Who would suspect they're being followed?" Mary wondered aloud.

"You never know," I told them. I didn't want anything to go wrong with this stakeout.

The pink Miata headed across town and we followed it, trying to stay at least a few car lengths behind it. The Miata didn't come to a complete stop once until it reached our high school parking lot.

"Why would she be stopping at school?" Dana wondered, peering through the windshield.

"Maybe she doesn't know that school is closed," Mary suggested.

I glanced at the inexpensive watch that was nearly cutting off the circulation in my arm. "It's near nine o' clock. If she was checking to see if school was open, she should have checked a lot earlier than this."

The girl with my body stepped out of the Miata and stared in the direction of the school. There were streams of yellow tape around certain areas of the parking lot. There weren't any police cruisers in sight, but the place was probably still under surveillance.

Patty got back into the car, circled around the parking lot, and pulled out into the street.

Dana had been wise enough not to pull into the parking lot. She'd continued driving and had stopped her car further down the street. Now, she pulled into someone's driveway and turned the car around so that we could continue tailing the pink Miata.

"My leg is falling asleep," Mary complained at some point during the drive.

It dawned on me that this stakeout wouldn't be enough for me. As entertaining as it was to have Dana, Mary, and Stephanie here, I needed to get closer to the action. I didn't just want to look from afar. I needed to get closer to Patty. I needed to find out how she was able to switch our bodies this way.

The answer seemed to present itself to me. The pink Miata parked in front of a store called Hidden Treasures. I'd never really noticed it before. It had to be a relatively new store. Someone was standing in the doorway. She looked over the top of the car at the person standing in the doorway.

The person in the doorway smiled at her and nodded in recognition. I couldn't tell whether it was a man or woman from this distance, but Patty followed the person into the store after a brief exchange of words.

I unlocked the passenger side door to Dana's car and opened it.

"What are you doing?" Dana hissed.

"I have to go in," I told her.

"She's going to see you!" Mary exclaimed.

I shook my head. "I have to go in," I insisted.

"At least wait until she leaves the store," Stephanie advised.

"Then we'd lose track of her," Dana said, throwing up her hands frustration.

"Not if you guys leave without me," I said slowly.

Dana frowned.

"I'm serious. You guys can follow her to her next destination, come back and pick me up, and we can go on from there." I frantically looked out the window in the direction of the store. "Or if you guys want to end the stakeout here, I understand, but I need to go into the store right now."

She must have seen the desperation in my eyes, because she finally nodded her head. "We'll continue to follow her after she leaves the store," she said. "But we'll come back to pick you up."

"Thanks," I said before leaping out of the car and lurching myself across the street, in the direction of Hidden Treasures.

I cupped my hands around my eyes and looked through the window on the door. No one was in sight. I pulled the door open. There was a bell attached to the door, and the tinkling of the bell announced my arrival.

"I'll be right with you," promised a deep voice.

I tiptoed through the store until the sound of low voices reached my ears. One of the voices was familiar; it was my own voice. The other voice was unfamiliar to me.

"It was amazing," Patty was saying. "I couldn't believe it."

"All of the items here are extremely powerful," the male voice responded. "One shouldn't underestimate any of them. You were probably not a believer when you walked into this store, but I am willing to bet that you are one now."

"Definitely."

"I am glad to have a happy customer," he said. "Are you looking for anything in particular today?"

"I want to find out how I can prevent someone from reversing this," she answered readily.

I ducked down to the floor, shamelessly eavesdropping on their conversation.

"The only thing you need is the book that you already have," the man said, turning and leading the teenager down the aisle. He was leading her further into the store.

I moved out of the aisle I'd been hiding in and got as close to them as possible, hiding behind a row of jelly-filled jars.

"I just want to warn you that the magic you are dealing with is very powerful. Use it carefully and without malice. If you fail to do either, you would be risking your life. Keep the book close to you at night and the details of what you must do will come to you in your dreams. You must follow each step precisely, or else all of your efforts will be wasted."

I heard everything he was saying, but I didn't understand a word of it. She must have though, because she took what he offered her and carried it with her to the front of the store, where the register was located.

For the first time since I'd been there, I started to pay attention to the items on the shelves around me. There were a lot of books, and jars filled with powder, jelly, and oils. There were candles in a bunch of different shapes. One of the candles was black and shaped like a skull. I had to cover my mouth to keep from screaming. What would a girl my age be doing roaming around a store like this?

The mysterious man rang up Patty's purchase and she left the store. The telltale ring of the bell above the door announced her departure. I started walking on my tiptoes again, looking around the store, when I nearly collided with the man who had been talking to Patty. He had long, flowing platinum blonde hair and frosty blue eyes. He looked too beautiful to be real.

He took one look at me and offered a sympathetic smile. "So I'm going to guess that you want me to tell you how to get your body back," he said to me.

Dana picked me up, just as she had promised, but not until after I'd talked to Aidan Powers, the man who owned Hidden Treasures-if I could even *call* him a man. If I'd been passing him on the street, I'm not sure I would have known what to call him. His voice was unmistakably masculine. He dressed like a man, in pants and a button-down shirt. There was something about him that was feminine, though. I just couldn't put my finger on it.

It didn't really matter to me whether he was a man or a woman. I just cared about getting my body back. He cornered me in that aisle and told me that I had to get my hands on the book. I asked him which book I should be looking for. He said that I would know it when I saw it.

What kind of answer is that, really? How would I know what book to look for if I didn't know what book I was looking for? He had taken one look at me and instantly known the situation that I was struggling with. So why wasn't he offering more guidance than telling me to look for a book?

I begged and pleaded for him to give me more information. I even searched through all of the things that he sold. Apparently, Patty had come here and found what she needed. I was hoping to find something that could help me. I couldn't find anything, though. I found a lot of books without words in them. I found a lot of jars filled with questionable substances. He wouldn't tell me how to use any of the items that he sold, so there wasn't much I could do. I walked out of the store empty-handed.

Dana picked me up a few minutes later to update me on the fact that the little pink Miata had made another stop, this time at a police station.

What business would she have at the police station? There were so many questions that I had; I didn't have many of the answers. I sat in silence in the passenger seat of the car, staring out of the window as trees and mailboxes and other cars whizzed by me.

We reached the police station just as Patty was getting into the car.

"We're just in time," Mary announced unnecessarily.

I felt like calling the stakeout off. I wasn't in the mood to watch Patty prancing around in my body like she was showing it off. Watching her wasn't doing anything to help me.

I was just about ready to call the whole thing off when the Miata pulled into a familiar driveway. My *boyfriend's* driveway. I felt as if I couldn't breathe as I watched Patty bounce out of the car.

Zander came running out of the front door like a kid who was trying to catch the ice cream truck. He grabbed Patty and wrapped his arms around her. They kissed. It made me sick. I seriously felt nauseated. I wanted to puke, right there in Dana's car. My anger was dangerously close to hitting its boiling point.

They whirled around a couple more times, kissing and hugging, right out there on his family's front lawn-and in broad daylight! They didn't seem to care *who* saw them.

I can honestly say that I don't remember exactly what happened next. I was sitting in the car next to Dana with Mary and Stephanie gabbing behind me. All three of them seemed to be in awe of the makeout session that was happening in front of us. One minute I was in the car, and the next minute I was out of the car and stampeding Patty and Zander.

❀ chapter twelve ❀

Patty and I went tumbling around on the grass. I pulled at her hair and punched at her face. I didn't hold back. I've fought a few girls in my time, so I know how to protect myself. I pummeled her face and scratched at her arms and legs. I was screaming at the top of my lungs, pouring all of my frustration into beating her into a pulp.

She barely put up a fight. I figured, even for a chubby girl she had to at least know *how* to throw a punch. Even if you don't know how to land a perfect aim, you should still know how to attempt. She didn't even do that. She just sat there and took it.

Zander pulled me off of her with a lot of effort. I was still kicking and screaming, even as he pulled me off. "Patty, calm down!" he was shouting.

If I'd had any sense, I would have punched and kicked at him too. How dare he not be able to tell the difference between me and Patty Coben!

Patty was on the ground, nursing her wounds. "She's crazy!" she kept saying over and over again. "If you don't keep her away from me, my parents are going to press charges!"

"*Your* parents!" I cried. "Those are my parents, you witch!"

"Back up, let's back up for a minute," Zander said, pushing me farther and farther away from Patty. "What are you doing here?"

I stared at him blankly. I couldn't even come up with a suitable excuse for being at his house. I'm usually pretty good when it comes to lying, but my mind was a complete blank. I blinked a couple of times and shrugged. "I don't know," I said numbly.

He gave me a look that really scared me. It was like he was looking at a crazy person. It made me feel like I *was* a crazy person. I had just attacked another girl in a blind rage. That couldn't be normal. He sighed and settled his arm across my wide shoulders. "This is probably because of what happened at the Homecoming Dance, right?"

"I don't want to talk about that," I said.

"Okay, okay," he said. "But I really am sorry for that."

I shrugged. It didn't matter to me that he was sorry. He was apologizing to the wrong person, really.

Patty got to her feet, dusting off her miniskirt and straightening her red blouse. It was strange, looking at her in that moment. Even with the bloody nose and even with the welt darkening into her cheek, she was beautiful. And she was me. I was beautiful. I'd worried and stressed out over ever single calorie that I'd taken in. I'd looked at myself in the mirror and I automatically looked for the flaws that were visible. No matter how thin I was, there were always another few pounds that I could lose. But, looking at Patty in my body, I realized that I was beautiful just the way I was.

If only I'd realized that sooner instead of being insecure and taking out my insecurities on other people, I wouldn't be living this nightmare right now.

A single tear slid down my cheek.

She cocked her head to the side and gave me the same frank perusal, looking me up and down. I wonder if she realized the same thing about herself. I wonder whether she thought she was beautiful, or did she think that she was ugly because of people like me, who got on her case every day about her weight?

I suddenly felt horrible. Zander was talking to me and I couldn't hear anything he said, my devastation was so extreme.

He glanced over his shoulder at Patty with a half-shrug. "Maybe I should take you both to the hospital to get checked out."

I shook my head. "I don't need to go to a hospital," I said quickly.

"I don't either," Patty agreed.

"Are you sure?" he asked her, obviously worried for her health.

She nodded her head, leaning on him as if it hurt to stand.

"Patty!"

Both Patty and I turned our heads in the direction of the voice who'd called her name. Dana, Mary, and Stephanie, were headed in our direction on foot.

I saw the brief expression of longing in Patty's eyes when she saw her friends and decided to play with her emotions a little bit. "Hey guys," I greeted, going over to hug them.

"We were just on our way to see the new horror flick at the Cineplex," Dana said. "What are you doing here? And why do you look like you just kicked the crap out of someone?"

Patty's mouth set in a grim line.

I almost laughed. "It's a long story," I answered, "but I'd definitely like to see that movie with you guys."

I left with Dana, Mary, and Stephanie. I left without apologizing to Zander. I left without apologizing to Patty. They didn't deserve an apology from me. Patty deserved every punch, every kick, and every hair pull that I'd given her.

When Dana dropped me off at home, there was a boy waiting on the porch.

With narrowed eyes, Stephanie muttered, "I wonder what Ricky wants."

I squinted at Ricky. I didn't have a clue as to who he was. I got out of the car and waved goodbye to Dana, Stephanie, and Mary. Then I turned towards the porch.

Ricky was a tall, lanky boy with dark brown hair. He wore a pair of wire-rimmed glasses. I don't think I've ever found a boy with glasses cute. They always look nerdy to me, like the type of boys who would rather play a video game than take a girl out on a date.

He was looking at me like he knew me very well, though, and that caused me to stop in my tracks. I didn't know what he expected me to say to him. I didn't know how I was supposed to react to him being there.

"Hi," he said, breaking the silence.

"Hi," I returned cautiously, walking up to him.

He shuffled from foot to foot. He actually looked...shy. I didn't know that boys could be shy. "I just wanted to say I'm sorry for what I did to you."

What did you do to me? I wanted to ask, but of course that would have been silly. Obviously, what he did to me would have been unforgettable, especially with how apologetic he was. "I appreciate your apology."

He squinted at me. "Do you?"

I nodded. "Yes."

"I mean, we dated for a long time. To suddenly dump you without any explanation...I felt really bad after that."

Dated? My mind was racing. *Fatty Patty had had a boyfriend? And he'd dumped her?* Realization dawned on me. And not long after he had dumped her, Zander and I had come along and played that prank on her. "Oh my God," I said out loud.

"I know," Ricky hurried to explain. "And I do want to explain everything to you. I'm just not ready yet."

Everything he was saying was going through one ear and out the other, because I was imagining how Patty must have felt that night at the Homecoming Dance. She'd shown up with the most popular boy in school, she'd been voted Homecoming Queen thanks to the fact that I'd replaced the real votes with a bunch of phony ballots with her name scribbled on them. She was probably thinking that there was life after Ricky, and she could probably live it with Zander, when I popped out on the stage and destroyed that dream for her.

I suddenly felt sick to my stomach. Zander had dumped me once, last year. He'd called me inconsiderate and shallow and hadn't wanted anything else to do with me. I'd felt as if my heart had broken in two. I had told him so. He'd said, "I'm surprised you even *have* a heart," and walked away.

It had devastated me. I moped around for weeks. I hadn't wanted to hang out at the mall with my friends, who weren't really my friends anyway. At the first word that Zander was single, a lot of them went after him and flirted with him whenever they saw him. Real friends wouldn't do that. I hadn't had friends like Mary, Dana, and Stephanie. They were *true* friends. The girls on my cheerleading squad smiled in my face, but they often talked about me behind my back. I know they did. They probably still do.

Ricky was still talking, but I held up my hand. "I'm sorry," I said. "But there's something important that I really have to do." I turned and fled into the house, leaving him standing on the porch.

I ran upstairs into Patty's bedroom and closed the door behind me. There was a phone on the nightstand and I didn't hesitate in picking it up. I punched in the phone number to the private line I had at my family's house.

"Hello? This is Tabatha."

"Hi, Patty, it's me. I just wanted to say I'm sorry for everything. I didn't know you and Ricky broke up before Zander and I played the prank on you."

"I'm just kidding," the familiar voicemail greeting said. "I'm not really here. But I probably will be in a little while, so leave me a message and I'll definitely get back to you."

I slammed the phone down and collapsed on the bed.

At some point, I must have fallen asleep, because I woke up to the sound of the phone ringing. One eye opened and searched for the digital clock on the nightstand. It was past midnight. I fumbled around for the phone. I couldn't see it in the dark. My hand finally bumped into the phone. I lifted the receiver and said in a groggy voice, "Hello?"

"I see that you called me," said my voice. "What was it you wanted to tell me?"

Too stunned to speak, I rubbed my eyes and sat up.

"Did you want to apologize for assaulting me earlier?"

"You had that coming and you know it," I told her.

She giggled. "How has it been, being me?"

"Not that bad."

"You once told your friends if you ever got as fat I was, to end your misery by killing you."

It was an odd thing to say. Then again, this entire situation was odd.

"Why did you call me earlier?"

"To apologize for everything."

There was silence on the other end of the other line. "You wanted to apologize?"

"Yes."

"For...*everything*?"

"Yes. I didn't know that Ricky broke up with you before Zander and I played the prank on you," I went on. "If I had known..."

"If you had known, you would have...what...waited six months to play the prank on me? What would you have done differently?"

"I wouldn't have done it at all."

"You shouldn't have done it in the first place," she snapped in a voice so cold, it made me tremble. "You should have never messed with me, Tabby. I was nice to you. I never had a problem with you. And then you had to go and ruin everything. And now..." She was choking back sobs.

The receiver shook in my hand. The emotion in her voice caused tears to form in my eyes. "I'm so sorry," I whispered.

"Well, it's too late for being sorry," she said after clearing her throat. "Zander is my boyfriend now. He adores me. And your parents are starting to adore me, too."

"Don't you miss your family?" I asked, mostly out of curiosity. "Don't you miss Dana and Stephanie and Mary?"

"Sure, I miss them," she answered. "But as each day goes on, I miss them less and less. The old Patty died on that stage at the Homecoming Dance. I'm not that same ugly girl anymore. I'm the most popular girl in school now. And you…you will learn not to mess with me."

chapter thirteen

The following morning, the annoying little snot burst into Patty's room again. "Pick up the phone, Patty!" he shouted at the top of his lungs. "Someone wants to talk to you."

With my eyes narrowed into slits, I sat up in bed and glanced over at the clock on the nightstand. It was eight o' clock on a Saturday morning. Whoever was calling me had better be in a life or death situation.

I picked up the phone and it didn't take me long to realize that I wasn't far off the mark.

"Is this Patricia Coben?" were the first words out of the man's mouth.

I frowned and asked, "Who wants to know?"

"I'm Detective Warner with the VHPD. I was hoping you had some time to come into the station today."

"For what?"

"We just had a couple of questions we wanted to ask you in relation to the Shelly Woods incident."

"I don't see how I can help you with that," I told him. "Shelly and I weren't friends."

"That much is apparent," the detective said. "We have a witness account of an altercation between you and Ms. Woods during gym class."

I blinked my eyes slowly. Quite honestly, I wasn't even fully awake yet. It took a few minutes for me to understand what he was saying. I kept thinking of myself as Tabatha, and as Tabatha, I'd never had an altercation with Shelly. What was he talking about? Shelly had idolized me.

"I'm still trying to get a hold of your mother on her cell phone," the detective went on. "But as soon as I get in touch with her, I'm going to ask her to bring you to the station so that I can ask you a couple of questions. There's nothing to be worried about. We just want to get to the bottom of this."

You could probably imagine how pleased Mrs. Coben was to realize that her daughter was wanted for questioning relating to a teenage girl's murder. She'd been out running errands when the detective had finally contacted her.

I sat in the front seat of the inexpensive, plain-looking sedan. I stared out of the window as Patty's mother drove. Before long, she was pulling into the parking lot of the Vista Heights Police Department.

We walked into the small, cramped building. Mrs. Coben started to approach the front desk, but a tall, dark-haired man wearing a navy blue suit appeared and beckoned us over to his cluttered desk.

I'm not good with guessing ages, but I'd guess that he was around thirty-five years old. He was a good-looking guy if you were into guys that old. I prefer boys my own age.

He introduced himself as Detective Warner. He was very polite. He apologized for the inconvenience, but assured us that he just wanted to get to the bottom of the case. "We don't take murder lightly here in Vista Heights," he told us.

"Who *does* take murder lightly?" I wondered aloud.

Mrs. Coben and the detective both turned their eyes on me. Then Patty's mother turned to face the detective. "I don't mean to be rude, but could you please tell us what this is all about?"

The detective gestured to the chairs facing his desk. "Please have a seat," he said as he lowered into his chair. He folded his hands on top of the desk and leaned forward. "We've been calling in acquaintances of Shelly's. We're trying to find out who would have motive enough to kill her."

At that point, I figured that that was probably why Patty had gone to the police station the previous day. She'd probably been called in for questioning, just like I had been.

Mrs. Coben turned to look at me. "Did you even know Shelly?"

"We had a class or two together," I said with a shrug of my shoulders. "We weren't like…best friends or anything."

"But one of your classmates did say that you two had an argument some weeks back," the detective said, narrowing his eyes.

I had to remember that I was supposed to be Patty Coben. He'd mentioned the altercation while I was on the phone with him and it had confused me because it had been so early in the morning. When I was Tabatha, Shelly had worshipped the ground I walked on. But she'd despised Patty Coben on sight. And furthermore, Patty and Shelly *had* exchanged heated words after one of our gym classes. It had gotten pretty hostile, actually. Patty had almost thrown a punch at Shelly, until I'd intercepted.

Something in my brain clicked and my eyes widened. "Oh my God," I muttered.

"What was that?" the detective asked.

Mrs. Coben looked equally as interested in what I had to say.

I didn't pay either of them any attention. Shelly had gotten in a lot of people's faces, but during the past few weeks, she'd been increasingly horrible to Patty. She'd set her sights on making Patty's life a living hell, and had succeeded with flying colors.

And now that Patty was no longer in her body…now that she was in *mine*…what was stopping her from going on a cold-blooded rampage? After all, everyone loved Tabatha. No one would think twice about Tabatha being a murderer. But *Patty?* Patty Coben? She'd been humiliated just about every day of her life. Her Homecoming night had turned out to be one gigantic disappointment, thanks to yours truly.

"Patty is the killer," I whispered, temporarily forgetting where I was sitting.

Mrs. Coben's brows furrowed and the detective sat up straighter in his chair.

"What did you just say?" he demanded.

I blinked my eyes and ran a hand through my stringy, blonde hair. "Nothing."

"I distinctively heard you say 'Patty is the killer,'" Detective Warner said. "But what I don't understand is why you would use that choice of words. I mean...you *are* Patricia Coben. Right?"

I looked between the detective and Mrs. Coben. They were both on the edges of their seats waiting to hear the next words to come out of my mouth. I could break down and tell them the entire story. They'd probably have me hospitalized or put in one of those rubber rooms with a self-hug jacket, but at least the truth would be out there. My other option was to claim to be Patty and plead my innocence. Option one: go to the looney bin and pray that I get a couple of visitors once in while, or option two: lie until I get my body back, and then somehow finger the *real* Patty Coben as the killer.

I took a deep breath. "I didn't say 'Patty is the killer,'" I said slowly. A plan was forming in my mind. "I said, '*Tabby* is the killer.'"

"Tabby?" the detective asked, flipping through a small notepad that was on top of his desk. "Are you indicating that Tabatha Andrews killed Shelly Woods?"

"Shelly and Tabatha were always arguing," I said with a wave of my hand. "They were supposed to be friends, but they were always competing for everything, especially boys. And Tabatha can be really cold and calculating. Don't underestimate her. Most people look at her and see a nice, pretty girl, but she's a monster."

The detective sat back in his chair, fidgeting with his pen. I couldn't tell if he was buying it or not. The expression on his face was tight with concentration. "It's interesting that you're implicating Tabatha Andrews as the killer," he said, "because it's Tabatha who was implicating you as Shelly's murderer."

Not only had she stolen my body, my boyfriend, and my perfect life, but she was also trying to frame me for murder. I was trying to hold it all together, but every girl has her breaking point. I'd been set on putting the police on her trail because I'd been sure that if Tabatha Andrews was the main suspect in a murder, Patty would want to trade bodies with me again. I guess she'd figured that if Patty Coben was the main suspect in a murder, she wouldn't have to worry about us ever having to switch bodies again.

I finally realized that I couldn't depend on Patty wanting her old body back. She seemed to be enjoying my life enough to ruin my chances of getting it back. If I wanted to get my life, my body, and my boyfriend back, I was going to have to take it by force. To do that, I was going to have to start following the directions of the guy from the Hidden Treasures store. He'd told me that I needed to get my hands on a book of hers. I had to get my hands on that book, if it was the last thing that I did.

On Wednesday, the school opened. I sat huddled in the shower of the Girls' locker room. I'd been there all morning. It had been quiet all morning, because my gym period was the first gym period of the day. When I started to drift off, a steady stream of voices sounded on the other side of the locker room door. Then the door opened and the entire locker room was flooded with noise.

I sat with my knees drawn up. My arms were wrapped around my knees. I was praying that I wouldn't be discovered. How could I explain why I was sitting alone in a shower stall? I couldn't.

The voices in the locker room were loud, but there was one voice louder than the rest of them. It belonged to

Victoria Lumley. She was on the varsity cheerleading squad with me and I'd recognize her high-pitched voice anywhere. "So, how was your date with Zander last night, Tabs?"

I dared a peek around the corner of the shower stall. Patty was surrounded by girls as she was trying to put on her school P.E. uniform. She shrugged her shoulders. "It was all right," she answered.

"Where did you guys go?"

"Did he take you to Lookout Point?"

"You are so lucky to be going out with Zander."

"He's gorgeous"

"*So* gorgeous."

"You two make the most adorable couple."

"No one goes to Lookout Point anymore," Patty said, wrinkling her nose in annoyance. "We just hung out at his house and rented movies. And why are you so interested in my life anyway? Don't any of you have boyfriends?"

All of the gossipy girls looked as if they had been slapped in the face. The locker room got very quiet.

Patty tossed her hair over her shoulder. I tried not to focus on the fact that it was *my* hair, not hers, that she was tossing. "I know that I'm popular. I know that I'm pretty. But you guys keep circling around me and looking up to me and I don't know why. I'm just another teenager. I'm just like you. It's pathetic, really. I mean *God*. You all need to get your own lives and stop obsessing about mine."

After she walked out of the locker room, all of the other girls started chattering right away. What was *her* problem? Some of the girls speculated that things must not being going well with her and Zander if she was so quick to snap that way.

Even I had to wonder why she'd gone off the deep end. I thought that she was enjoying being me. Could she be having second thoughts?

I continued to huddle in the shower stall until the locker room was completely empty. Then, I crept out of the shower area and into the main locker room, where I'd seen Patty standing. A stylish Prada backpack sat on the floor in plain sight. I knelt to the floor and didn't hesitate in rummaging through it.

I rifled through the papers that were in the backpack. There were a couple of text books that were shoved in there. I never put heavy books into my Prada backpack. I always had someone carry my books for me. I didn't want the backpack to start bursting at the seams due to the uninteresting literature that our school forced us to read.

I unzipped the front compartment of the backpack and my hand brushed against a book...if you could call it that. It was pretty small and didn't have many pages. The front and back covers had no words or art on them. I flipped through it. Steps seemed to outline each page of the book. Before my eyes, the words on the book faded and each page turned blank.

Shocked, I flipped through the pages again. There were no longer words on any of the pages. *He said that I would know the book when I saw it,* I thought to myself. This had to be the book that he was talking about. I finally had my hands on it. Now I just had to figure out what to do with it.

Dana, Stephanie, and Mary all took me to our town's best pizza joint later on that night. I'd made the decision not to tell them that I'd been questioned by the police. I didn't want to worry them unnecessarily. I also made a conscious decision not to include them on the stakeouts anymore. Most likely, Patty was now a cold-blooded killer. I didn't want to get the girls involved.

Even though I was trying to distance myself from them, they still insisted on taking me out that night. They were such loyal friends. A girl had to be crazy to give up friends like these.

I hadn't had pizza in years, so I was excited about that alone. Pizza has the most ungodly amount of carbs *ever*. I felt like I was gaining weight by just *looking* at pizza, let alone eating it. That was the old me, anyway. The new me was going to enjoy the pizza that we ordered. The new me had a whole new batch of priorities.

Dana, Stephanie, and I were at the point of begging Mary not to include anchovies on our pizza when the double doors swung open and Tabatha walked into the place with a dark-haired boy on her arm. Only the boy on her arm wasn't Zander; it was Ricky Kellerman.

Dana stopped in mid-sentence and stared at the pair.

Stephanie fidgeted nervously in her seat, probably wondering how I would react.

Mary's menu barely made a sound as it fell to the table.

And my jaw dropped…to the floor.

chapter fourteen

Patty's arm was linked through Ricky's as they approached a booth across the room and claimed it. I don't think she'd spotted me. If she had, she'd probably have claimed the booth right behind ours just to spite me and rub it in my face.

The question on everyone's mind seemed to be, *Why is she with Ricky Kellerman?* Where was Zander and did he know that she was out with another boy? Everyone in the restaurant seemed to turn their focus on the girl who appeared to be Tabatha. A couple of teenagers brought out their cell phones so they could snap pictures of the couple who seemed blissfully unaware of everything that was going on around them.

I turned to face Dana, Stephanie, and Mary. They were all staring at me wide-eyed, wondering why I hadn't had a nervous breakdown yet. "I have to get closer to their table," I told them.

Dana and Mary exchanged glances. "You're kidding, right?" Mary asked.

I shook my head, already collecting my purse.

"We can't all go over there," Stephanie reasoned. "She'll recognize us."

"And if you go over there, she'll probably recognize you," Dana pointed out.

They were right. Even if I chose a booth and sat with my back to her, she would probably know herself enough to know that it was me sitting next to her. The sad fact is that I knew myself well enough to know that I would take that risk. "I have to try," I told them, standing up from the booth.

I spotted the perfect booth to eavesdrop from. The heavens must have been on my side for a divine miracle such as this, because there was a huge, gaudy floral arrangement that was on the back-end of Patty's booth. I could sit in the booth right next to her without much worry of being spotted. Keeping my face turned from them as much as possible while walking by, I claimed the booth and exhaled with relief once I was seated,

"The service here is horrible," Patty was complaining to Ricky. "It takes about half an hour for the staff to even notice you're here."

"It's one of my favorite places in town," Ricky said. He paused for a moment, then asked, "Why are we here?"

"Because you wanted to come here," she answered.

"I don't mean that. I mean...why are you here with me?"

Great question, I thought to myself, tempted to peek through the floral nightmare.

"I've been watching you for quite awhile," she told him. "A couple of times, I wanted to talk to you, but you always looked so busy."

"*I* looked busy?" he asked incredulously. "You're the head cheerleader and you're the president of most of the school clubs here."

This time I did chance a peek at them. I parted some of the leafy plants so that I could visually see her reaction to his words.

She shrugged her shoulders. "None of that matters."

"Do you need a tutor or something? Is that why I'm here?"

"Don't be stupid," she sneered at him. "My grades are probably better than yours are. You're here because I want you to be. I've...liked you. For a long time."

"You're dating Zander, though."

"Will you please stop bringing up topics that don't matter?"

I couldn't piece together why she would want to bring him here. He had dumped her, hadn't he? And she was telling him that she liked him? Did she think that she would have another chance with him, since she was me? And if so, what would that prove?

When a waiter appeared, she ordered a large pizza with mushrooms, pepperoni, spinach, olives, and peppers. Then she arched a look at Ricky. "Did you want to add anything to that?"

He shook his head slowly. When the waiter scurried off to give the chef their order, he turned to Patty. "You just ordered my favorite kind of pizza."

She offered him a flirtatious smile. "Did I really?"

He sat back in his seat, looking as confused as I felt.

She abandoned her seat and slid next to him. He looked like he might faint. I had to cover a giggle with my hand. He looked so uncomfortable, it was comical.

That was how it went for most of the time they were there. She mercilessly flirted with him and he kept shrinking away from her, not quite knowing how to handle her. Throughout the meal, she would keep running her fingers through his hair or she'd set her hand on his thigh.

Towards the end of the meal, she asked him, "Your mom works tonight, right?"

He blinked and stared at her in the strangest way. "How did you know that?"

She shrugged. "I've got my ways. Since she's working, then the house will be all ours. You should take me there. Now."

Even as weird as the situation was, he was still a teenage boy. He was still a bundle of raging hormones. So of course he didn't turn her down. He was physiologically *unable* to turn her down. She was me, after all.

They had their leftovers boxed up. I hadn't ordered anything and it didn't look as if I'd be able to. Naturally I had to follow them. I had to see what she was up to. So as they gathered everything together, I slipped out of the booth and told Dana, Stephanie, and Mary that I was heading off.

When they asked me where, I didn't even bother to lie to them. "I'm going to follow them," I told them.

Mary started objecting right away, but Dana quieted her down. "You're not going without us," Dana said sternly.

I guess that's what friends are for.

We packed everything up. They'd ordered pizza as soon as I had left the booth. We all piled into Dana's car and I chomped on a couple of pizza slices in one of the Styrofoam boxes they'd designated for me.

We started tailing the familiar pink Miata. The Miata led us to a dark, two-story house that was isolated on its side of the block. There weren't any houses on either side of it. This wasn't my family's house, so I was going to guess that it was Ricky's. And evidently, Ricky's family had money, because the house that was towering over us had to have cost a pretty penny.

Dana parked down the street and shut off the headlights to the car. We were going to have to walk the rest of the way and pray that the Kellermans didn't have an expensive security system that would alert anyone inside the house that we were stalking around the property.

We crept up to the driveway just as Ricky was letting Patty inside the house. He closed the door behind them, and we could tell which direction they were moving in by the lights that were turned on. Patty's friends and I moved alongside the house and were greeted with a large picture window. A dim light was turned on and it seemed we were peering into the living room. There was a sheer gold curtain over the window, but we could see right through it.

Ricky gestured for Patty to have a seat. We couldn't hear a word that either of them was saying. The windows were closed tightly. All we could do was guess by reading their body language.

Patty crooked her finger at him and he went over to her. He sat down next to her. As shy as he had seemed with me several nights ago, he didn't seem to be shy now. He leaned into Patty, ducked his head down, and kissed her.

I cringed when I saw them kiss. Even though it wasn't really me kissing him, the girl kissing him looked just like me.

Dana, Stephanie, and Mary started talking instantly. I shushed them down with a wave of my hand and continued to watch the couple in the living room.

Ricky pulled Patty onto his lap and wrapped his arms around her. Then they kissed again. She broke off the kiss and leaned down to whisper something in his ear. He looked confused. She whispered something else, and he nearly pitched her off of his lap.

"Oh my God," Mary whispered, covering her mouth.

"What's going on?" Dana demanded.

Ricky stood from the couch with his eyes wide. He seemed to be afraid of Patty. *Did she tell him the truth?* I couldn't help but wonder. *Did she tell him that she's not really Tabatha, that she's really Patty Coben, the girl that he dumped?*

She crooked her finger at him again. He was staring at her warily, but he did start walking towards her. As he drew closer to her, he started talking. He was probably apologizing for dumping her or something.

She smiled at him and tilted her head to the side. Then she opened her arms as if she wanted to hug him.

He stepped into her embrace, still talking. His lips were still moving. She angled an arm behind her back.

I grew tense.

"What is she doing?" Stephanie asked.

I shook my head, speechless and clueless. I didn't know what Patty was doing.

She reached beneath the hem of the cream-colored Banana Republic shirt that she was wearing. When her hand came back into view, something glimmered in it.

"Is that a knife?" Dana murmured.

Without hesitation, Patty raised the glimmering object and plunged it into Ricky's back. She withdrew the object, and then drove it into Ricky's back again. He stumbled away from her, with the sliver of steel still protruding out of his back.

"Oh my God," Mary whispered again, and turned away from the grotesque scene.

"She just stabbed him!" Dana shouted. "Tabatha just stabbed Ricky!"

"Stephanie, let me see your cell phone," I demanded.

Once she handed over the cell phone, I punched in the numbers 9-1-1. A female operator answered. I interrupted her by shouting, "We need an ambulance at the corner of Street and Macher Drive! And we need one now. A person has been stabbed multiple times."

"What is your name?" the operator asked.

"I don't have time for that. Get an ambulance here ASAP and connect me with Detective Warner."

chapter fifteen

None of us wanted to spend the night alone after witnessing Patty's attack on Ricky. Dana's hands shook as she drove us back to the Coben residence. "If Tabatha's out there exterminating people, then you're probably on her list," she had said. "After all, you did attack her last weekend."

She had a point. And not only that, but I was the one person who knew that she wasn't really Tabatha Andrews. That had to be motive enough to kill me. When she'd gone to Hidden Treasures, she'd asked for a way to make sure that this switch couldn't be reversed. A permanent way to make sure of that would be to kill me. It seemed that she was opting to frame me for murder and put me in jail for the rest of my life. That wasn't such a bad idea, either. Either way, she'd get to continue living *my* life as Tabatha.

She was sneaky. I had to hand it to her. Before all of this started happening, I would have never thought Fatty Patty capable of a plan so vile. She always seemed like a sweet, nice girl. Now, she was a monster. And it was most likely my fault. I'm sure she hadn't forgotten that. There was no way she'd let *me* forget it.

She'd first murdered Shelly Woods, a girl she'd had an argument with. Then, she killed Ricky, the boy who had dumped her. It was the perfect frame, because while she got to kill off her frustration (*literally*), I was the one who would be suffering the consequences.

Detective Warner had told me not to leave the Kellerman's residence. He'd wanted me to wait until he got there. I refused to be a sitting duck, though. I told him that if he had any questions, he knew where to find me.

Dana and Stephanie stayed with me that night. We had to drop Mary off because she had very strict parents that wouldn't let her stay out on a weeknight. Dana didn't want to leave my side. She couldn't believe what we'd all seen and she couldn't make sense of it. That night, she talked my ear off, trying to come up with reasons as to why "Tabatha" might want to kill Ricky.

"I could understand why *you* would want to kill Ricky," she said. "After all, he dumped you. But he was like putty in her hands. Why would she want to kill him?"

I shrugged my shoulders. "She's a psychopath. Psychos don't need to have a method to their madness."

"But they often do," Dana reasoned, chewing on her bottom lip.

Stephanie shrugged. "Either way, can we get some sleep? We do still have to go to school tomorrow, you know."

"How can you sleep at a time like this?" Dana demanded. "We're being picked off one by one!"

Eventually Dana calmed down, but she was right. How could anyone sleep after having seen what we'd seen? I didn't know if Ricky was going to be okay. I didn't even know if the ambulance had gotten there in time. If they'd been too late though, that would mean that Patty had killed two people. At what point would she stop? And who was next on her list?

Thursday morning, the rumor mills were churning. After putting up an admirable fight, Ricky had passed away in the wee hours of the morning. His wounds had been too severe. He'd had a slim chance of recovery; as night had slowly turned into morning those chances had gone from slim to none. A makeshift memorial was set up in front of the school, and pictures of Ricky and Shelly had been posted.

Students would stop by and scrawl something on the bulletin board or light one of the candles.

Everyone was solemn. Halloween decorations adorned the halls, but I couldn't even get excited about that. Detective Warner hadn't tried to contact me and I was wondering whether or not he was taking my allegations seriously.

I stood in the Girls' bathroom, staring into the mirror. The door opened, but I paid no attention. I was too lost in my own thoughts.

"Poor Ricky," a familiar voice said.

I turned to face Patty. "Are you going to try to kill me too?" I challenged.

She tilted her head to the side, halted at a mirror, and ran a hand through her long, dark hair. She admired herself and then turned to me. "Do you think I'm putting on a little weight?" she teased.

I rolled my eyes.

"And anyway, Ricky was pathetic. No one cared about him, not even his parents. His parents cared about him as much as my parents cared about me." She adjusted her orange long-sleeved knit top as she turned to face me. "He dumped me and didn't tell me why…that is, until last night."

I didn't say anything. I couldn't.

"I told him who I really was. At first, he didn't believe me. But he had to. I knew things that no one else would know. And after I told him who I was, he started apologizing. It was *so* sad. I mean…I felt sorry for him for a second, you know?" She dug into her purse and fished out a piece of gum, which she popped into her mouth. "I almost didn't go through with it. I mean he was so pathetic, I should have just let him continue living his meaningless little life."

"Why didn't you?" I dared to ask.

"Because of the master plan, silly," she said, closing the distance between us and slinging an arm around my shoulders. She wheeled the both of us around so that we were standing side by side facing the mirror. Our reflections seemed oddly out of place in the mirrored glass. I was wearing her face and she was wearing mine. "If I'm framing you for murder, then I have to make sure to kill all of the people dear to you, who *hurt* you...I mean, me." She threw her head back and laughed.

I pushed her away from me. "Don't touch me," I warned.

She placed an index finger against her lips. "Shh. I won't tell anybody if you won't. Remember, keep this just between us, okay?" She glanced at herself in the mirror again, ran a hand through her hair, and exited the bathroom.

I watched her leave. She'd admitted that she was framing me. And she'd said that she had to kill everyone who had hurt her. Who could she possibly go after next?

And then her words came to me, the words she had said to me on the phone when she'd called me that night. *"The old Patty died on that stage at the Homecoming Dance."*

I couldn't be sure, but I thought I knew who her next victim would be. And I had to stop her.

Dana, Stephanie, and Mary all faced me. We had all met up at Dana's house. I told them that there was something important that I needed to tell them.

When everyone was present and accounted for, I started to tell them *everything*. I started from the day that I'd been late to school and had to go to in-school detention. I told them how I'd bumped into Patty and how I'd made the now infamous remark about ending my misery if I ever got that fat. I didn't hold anything back, not even my most shameful moments. I told them that I was not Patricia Coben. I was Tabatha Andrews, and by some cruel twist of fate, I was in Patty's body. And furthermore, Patty currently possessed my body.

When I was finished talking, the room grew quiet. None of them knew what to say or how to respond. Dana, as always, was the first to react. She burst out laughing.

I sighed and turned my back to them.

"You can't expect us to believe that, Patty," Mary said in a quiet voice.

I whirled on them all. "I'm not Patty, okay! I'm not Patricia. I'm not Pat. I'm not Patty. I'm not *Fatty* Patty. I'm Tabatha, Tabby if you're close friends with me."

Mary looked hurt.

I rolled my eyes and shook my head. "Look, I know it sounds crazy. But she's trying to frame me for murder. She killed Shelly, who crossed paths with her. She killed Ricky, who dumped her. And she and I are the only people who know that I'm not really her and she's not really me. I think she's going to try to kill Zander because of the prank that we pulled on her on Homecoming night. I can't let her do that. I have to stop her."

Even Dana looked startled at my words.

"I'm not asking you to believe me. But I needed to tell you the truth so that you could help me. So that you could know what we're dealing with." I took a deep breath. "She told me that she's not Patty anymore. She said that Patty died that night at the Homecoming Dance."

All three of them were looking at each other, wondering if they should take me seriously.

"Are you going to seriously tell me that you haven't noticed I've been acting strangely lately?" I finally shouted.

"You have been acting very strangely," Dana said. "But what you're telling us is crazy."

"I don't disagree with you," I said, wrapping my arms around myself. "I'm ashamed of the things that I said to her and about her. I'm ashamed of how I treated her. It took a lot for me to realize this, but everyone is beautiful. Everyone shines in their own way. Patty used to be a funny, happy girl, and I took that away from her. I made her the monster that she is now. And I have to make things right."

They told me that they would help me. They looked concerned for my mental well-being, but they did say they'd help me.

And later that night, I had a nightmare. I usually didn't remember my nightmares, but I remembered this nightmare vividly. I confronted Patty and we started to fight. I wanted my body back and she wanted to kill me. I don't remember who won the fight, but when I sat up in bed and looked over to the nightstand, the pamphlet was in plain sight. I picked it up and flipped to the first page. Before tonight, all of the pages had been blank, but now there were words scribbled across the front page in what looked like my own handwriting.

Step 1: Obtain a strand of her hair

I held the book to my chest and blinked in the dark. I started all of this with my rudeness and with my insecurity. It was up to me now. I had to end this.

part three
the showdown

chapter sixteen

Patricia drew a brush through her long, dark hair. She stared into the mirror and admired the image that she saw there. She liked living life as Tabatha Andrews. Everyone loved her. She had money to spare. She dated the boy that every other girl in school wanted to date. Life didn't get much better than this.

And yet, she was always living in fear that this would be snatched away from her. She was always living in fear that Tabatha would somehow reverse all of this and banish her to living life as Patty Coben again.

Over my dead body, she thought to herself now as she brushed her hair.

"Are you ever going to come over here, babe?" Zander called from behind her.

She dropped her brush on his dresser and turned to face him. His parents had gone out of town, so they'd had the house to themselves for the past few days. For the past few days, she'd let him have his way with her. He was a good kisser. He was so loyal. In a sense, he was just as pathetic as Ricky was.

Boys kept groveling at her feet and putting her on a pedestal because of how she looked. It didn't matter how cruel or nasty she was to them. It was so sad, really.

She walked over to him and ran her fingers through his hair, exactly as she had run her hand through Ricky's hair. He stood up from the bed and wrapped his arms around her.

She continued ruffling his hair as she asked him, "Do you sometimes think that we went way too far with what we did to Patty at the Homecoming Dance?"

"You know I do," he murmured as he nuzzled against her cheek. "I've told you that several times."

"So why did you do it, then?" she asked him.

"Because you wanted me to."

"You would break a girl's heart like that just because I asked you to?" she wondered aloud.

"I already have."

"And you don't feel guilty or anything?"

He pulled away from her and looked down at her. "You've been acting different lately," he said. "Are you feeling all right?"

She shrugged her shoulders. "I'm just curious. Not many high school boys are as loyal as you are."

"You know how much I like you. I'd do anything for you."

"Anything?" she questioned.

This time it was his turn to shrug his shoulders. "Anything," he repeated.

"Good," she said, and hugged him again.

The next day was uneventful for the most part. Patty seemed to misplace her hairbrush during gym class. The cheerleaders buzzed about the state championships they'd have to attend soon.

For the past few weeks, she'd been letting the other cheerleaders integrate their own moves in their cheers. They had been pleasantly surprised when their cheerleading captain turned this new leaf, but she didn't know anything about cheering. Rather than humiliate herself, she let the other cheerleaders do all of the work. Then, she took the credit for it. She doubted that it was much different from what the real Tabatha did.

She never had to do homework or take notes. Other students did it for her. It was quite amazing, really. When Tabatha had claimed to be the Queen of Vista Heights High, she hadn't been exaggerating. People were constantly tripping over themselves to accommodate her. They'd put so much effort into just being able to greet her in the morning when she entered the school. Even though Patty couldn't help but enjoy it, it also sickened her that everyone treated her the way they did just because of how she looked.

She'd tried to be as nasty and snotty as possible to the people around her, but they didn't care. She could be as snobby as she wanted to be, and people forgave her for it. She wished she had the guts to take responsibility for the murders of Shelly and Ricky. Maybe everyone in Vista Heights would have given her an award for being so pretty. Then maybe they would have gotten her a pair of fuzzy pink handcuffs so she didn't hurt her pretty little wrists while she was rotting away in prison-*if* they even put her there. Maybe she wouldn't even get convicted of murder.

She'd plead innocent, and the jury would let her off the hook because she was just too pretty to go to jail.

When she was Patty Coben, she hadn't been pretty, but she'd had fun. She'd had a good life. She'd taken her family for granted sometimes, but she did love her family and she missed them. She definitely missed her friends and wished that she could gab with them over pizza.

Once in awhile, she would cry. She'd cry for herself and for what she'd done to Shelly and Ricky. Once in awhile, she would hate the image that greeted her in the mirror. She'd wish that she could go back to the way her life used to be.

But then she'd drag a brush through her hair and she'd get over it. She wasn't Patty Coben anymore. She was Tabatha Andrews. And everyone loved her.

Tabatha sat in Patty's room, dangling Patty's brush in the air. Tangled strands of dark hair were laced throughout the bristles of the brush. The pamphlet had instructed her to get strands of Patty's hair and she'd been successful. She'd stayed behind again in gym class and had plucked the brush out of the other girl's backpack.

The only question was: what should she do with the brush now? The other pages in the pamphlet were still blank. With a sigh, she set the brush on the nightstand and climbed into bed. She'd been tempted to follow Patty and Zander after school. She couldn't let harm come to Zander, because it would all be her fault. The only reason he'd been cruel to Patty is because she had ordered him to.

In the end, though, she realized that she couldn't watch over Patty and Zander every minute of the day. Besides, she had to obey the pamphlet and keep an eye out for any new instructions it would give to her. Something told her that following the directions in the pamphlet was her best bet.

She had trouble sleeping again. She sank into a restless sleep, where she had a nightmare.

She was staring into a mirror with her hands braced on either side of the sink. She was still in Patty's body, but when she looked into the mirror, she saw the face of Tabatha. She peered closer and closer into the mirror.

Without warning, the image of Tabatha leapt out of the mirror and lunged for her, clawing at her throat. When the mirror image of Tabatha spoke, she spoke in Patty's voice. "You're never going to get your body back, do you hear me? Never!"

Tabatha bolted upright, blindly grasping for the lamp on the nightstand. The room was bathed in light. She didn't dare look towards the mirrored vanity in the corner of the room, but nothing looked to be out of place. She opened the nightstand drawer and her hand bumped into what she was looking for: the pamphlet.

She flipped to the second page, and just as she'd expected, there was a second step.

Step 2: Embrace your rage

Her heart was racing as she read the words in the booklet. She didn't quite understand what the words meant. She knew what rage was. She definitely wasn't a stranger to that emotion. But how was she supposed to embrace it? Those words could be interpreted a number of ways.

She closed the book and sat on her bed, lost in thought.

chapter seventeen

Saturday morning was bleak. The sun was covered by elongated clouds, so the sky was a drab, gray color. It looked as if it might rain at any moment. Beneath the clouded sky, family and friends of Ricky Kellerman were grieving. A priest droned on in a long speech about the importance of life and celebrating the beginning and the end of life.

Ricky's parents couldn't bring themselves to look at the priest or the casket mounted above a gaping hole in the ground. Mrs. Kellerman in particular could barely keep her wits about her. Her racking sobs nearly drowned out the sound of the priest's voice.

A crowd of grievers surrounded the polished oak casket, dressed in formal black clothing. Tabatha was present, as were Stephanie, Mary, and Dana. They were all leaning on each other for support. It was difficult for them to look at the casket without remembering what they'd witnessed the night Ricky was attacked by Patty.

A lot of their classmates were there. The moment she'd shown up with her friends, several of their classmates had started whispering to each other. They were most likely telling each other that she was Patty Coben, Ricky's former girlfriend. They most likely pitied her when the truth was, out of everyone here she probably knew Ricky the least.

The funeral dragged on. When the casket started to lower into the ground, Mrs. Kellerman buried her face into her husband's shoulder to stifle her sobs. Then, she unexpectedly broke away from her husband and headed towards the casket as if she were going to throw herself on top of it.

Tabatha clapped a hand over her mouth and Dana tugged on her arm as if to say, *"Can you believe what we're seeing?"*

Thankfully, Mr. Kellerman surged forward in time to hold his wife back. He attempted to murmur comforting words into her ear, but she screamed at him.

"No, Steve, okay? He's our son! Our son! Our baby boy!" Her hands balled into fists and she backed away from her husband. She turned around in a small circle, eyeing everyone who was in the crowd gathered around the casket. "Someone killed our child in our very own house! How can I stand by and pretend like it didn't happen?"

Mr. Kellerman didn't have an answer to that question. No one did.

"I want to know who killed my boy, my Ricky," Mrs. Kellerman stated in a surprisingly level voice.

Low murmurs ran through the crowd at Mrs. Kellerman's words.

Just then, Tabatha spotted Patty and Zander standing on the other side of Ricky's grave. They were holding hands and speaking to each other in low tones. Tabatha wondered how long they'd been there; this was her first time seeing them.

With a long, final look at her husband, Mrs. Kellerman stalked off, towards a sleek limousine with tinted windows.

The flustered priest tried his best to close the ceremony with encouraging words. Some of Ricky's classmates stepped forward and dropped roses onto his casket. Patty was one of those individuals. She was dressed in an expensive black slip of a dress. Stylish sunglasses hid her eyes from view, but her lips were painted a daring shade of red. She knelt to the ground and dropped several roses onto Ricky's casket. Then her lips started to move. Was she talking to Ricky?

Tabatha started inching forward before she could stop herself.

"I'm sorry, baby, but you deserved it," Patty was saying in a low voice. "You deserved it, but I'm sorry."

"I think I'm going to be sick," Tabatha whispered, covering her mouth with her hand.

Dana glanced past Tabatha with narrowed eyes. "I know what you mean," she muttered. "Are you going to the Kellermans'? They're having a get-together at their house."

"I don't think I can handle that," Tabatha told her. "I really don't. Not after seeing his mom breaking down like that."

"You have to," Stephanie chimed in. "You dated him for two years. Well…not you, I guess. But Patty did. And Patty got along well with his mom, too. They're probably expecting you to show up."

Tabatha could think of at least ten reasons why she *shouldn't* go to the Kellermans' residence, but Stephanie brought up an interesting point. Patty was setting her up for murder and it would seem more suspicious if she didn't show up to pay her respects to her ex-boyfriend's family. With a sigh of resignation, she followed Dana, Stephanie, and Mary to Dana's car.

When Tabatha showed up to the Kellermans' residence, she discovered that irony doesn't just happen in the movies. Ricky's friends and family were gathered in the family room, where he'd been attacked. It also seemed as if everyone started whispering once she entered the room. Was she imagining things?

She entered the room uneasily, fidgeting with the hem of the black blouse that she wore. Patty's friends weren't able to attend the gathering with her. She was on her own.

Unable to deal with the whispering, she slipped out of the family room and into a narrow hallway. She pressed her back against the wall. She only had to pay her respects.

right? Technically that meant that she could walk up to Mr. and Mrs. Kellerman, express her sympathy for their loss, and leave. She didn't actually have to stay here for a significant period of time, did she?

"Supposedly, Fatty Patty's lost it," said an unfamiliar masculine voice.

Tabatha froze.

"Ricky dumped her a few days before the Homecoming Dance and then Zander played that cruel prank on her. And then Tabatha went out on a date with Ricky. I heard Patty's totally lost it. She was probably crazy with jealousy."

"But do you think she was crazy enough to kill him?" a female voice questioned.

Two people in the family room were discussing the possibility of Patty being Ricky's killer. Everyone at the funeral who'd been whispering hadn't been sympathizing with Tabatha, because they thought she was Patty. They were whispering because they thought she was a cold-blooded killer.

"And the other girl who was killed, Shelly…Patty had an argument with her a few weeks before she was murdered. Isn't that creepy?"

"I can't believe she even showed up to his funeral."

"How disrespectful," the feminine voice agreed.

Tabatha whirled around and nearly collided with Patty. "What are you doing here?" she demanded.

Patty shrugged. "I could probably ask you the same thing, since everyone suspects you of killing Ricky."

"Why would I kill Ricky? I didn't even know him."

"Not according to everyone else. According to everyone else, you dated him for two years, before he dumped you." With those words, Patty turned as if to leave.

Tabatha stalked behind her with her hands placed on her wide hips. She followed Patty into a bright, empty kitchen with an entire wall of windows. "You don't actually think you're going to get away with this, do you?"

"In a sense, I already have. It's only a matter of time."

Those words sent a chill racing up Tabatha's back. It was then that she realized that Patty wasn't going to stop. She wasn't going to stop killing people and tormenting her until she got what she wanted. She was heartless and manipulative. When she'd said that the old Patty had died the night of the Homecoming Dance, she hadn't been speaking in a figurative sense. She was truly someone else now, completely changed.

Patty tilted her head to the side and clucked her tongue. "Are you all right? You look like you might be coming down with something."

"I'm fine."

"Are you sure?" Patty asked, closing the distance between them.

Several hours later, Tabatha wouldn't know what came over her in that instant. A flash of red shone behind her eyes and before she knew it, she was on top of Patty, bashing her face in with her fists.

Patty's screams must have alerted some of the people in the family room, because suddenly the kitchen was full of confused people chattering and muttering.

"What is going on?" shouted a demanding voice. Mr. Kellerman soon appeared at the front of the gawking audience. His eyes widened at the sight of the two teenagers fighting on his kitchen floor. He pulled the heavyset girl off of the dark-haired cheerleader with an expression of concern on his face.

The cheerleader's face was bruised and the skin had been broken over the crests of her cheeks. "We've got to get you to a hospital," he murmured. Then, he angled his gaze over to Tabatha. "What the hell got into you?"

The dark-haired cheerleader sat on the floor, covering her face with both hands. "Patty's crazy!" she cried. "First she killed Shelly. Then she killed Ricky. And now she wants to kill me!"

"Oh my God," someone said from the doorway to the kitchen.

Mr. Kellerman's brows knit with concern as he stared at the chubby blonde girl.

She stared down at the floor, looking defeated. She didn't know what had gotten into her. Could that be what the pamphlet meant by embracing her rage?

chapter eighteen

Mr. Kellerman called the police and Tabatha was hauled away to the Vista Heights Police Department for questioning. Detective Warner didn't look pleased to see her. If it was possible, he actually managed to look just as frazzled as she did.

"Do you ever stay out of trouble?" he asked her when he entered the interrogation room.

She shrugged her shoulders.

"You've got some serious allegations going on here. It seems your classmates suspect you of murdering Shelly and Ricky."

"Are you arresting me?" she asked him quietly.

He sighed and sat down at the table, claiming the chair across from hers. "I don't want to," he said slowly, "but you're going to have to be honest with me. A lot more honest than you've been lately."

"If I *was* honest with you, you wouldn't believe me," she told him.

"Do you mind if I record this?" he asked her.

She shrugged her shoulders. "No, I don't mind."

He withdrew a tape recorder from his jacket pocket and set it on the table between them. After pressing a button on the recording device, he gestured for her to speak. "Try me."

She weighed the options that she had and figured that she had nothing to lose by telling him the truth. She started from the beginning and told him the entire story.

He stared at her with an expressionless gaze until she concluded the story. "We shouldn't have brought you into this interrogation room," he said finally.

A hopeful smile appeared on her face.

"We definitely shouldn't have brought you into this interrogation room," he repeated. "We should have taken you into a rubber room and slapped a strait jacket on you."

The smile was wiped from her face.

"You can't seriously expect me to believe that," he said, standing from his chair and pacing the length of the room. "That you're really Tabatha Andrews and the girl who is currently in Tabatha's body is Patricia Coben."

"You asked for the truth and I gave it to you," she said, shrugging.

He stared at her for several moments as if not knowing what to say. "You can't go around saying that you've switched bodies with one of your classmates, Patricia. I'm serious. Ricky Kellerman's parents won't hesitate to have you locked up. If not in jail, then in a psychiatric ward somewhere."

"I'm not crazy!" she shouted.

"You attacked Tabatha on the day of Ricky's funeral, *at* his parents' house!" he yelled back. "And now you're sitting here claiming that Tabatha isn't even Tabatha. You're claiming that she's you and you're her. That's impossible."

"What's possible and what's *im*possible isn't up to you," she said.

He ran a shaking hand through his hair. He appeared on edge. "I want to believe you, Patricia, I do. But you can't come to me with these whacky stories and expect me to take you seriously."

"Are you arresting me or not?"

"Your parents are on their way to pick you up."

She nodded, apparently satisfied with that answer.

"I'm just going to ask you one question."

"Okay."

"Did you kill Ricky Kellerman?"

"No."

"Did you kill Shelly Woods?"

"You said you were only going to ask one question."

"That question had a Part A and a Part B."

She rolled her eyes. "I haven't killed anyone, Detective Warner. You can believe me. You can choose not to believe me. I really don't care. I just know I'm not going to let Patty frame me for murder. And if you don't help me, then I'll just have to deal with her myself."

A light knock sounded on the door. Detective Warner glanced at the door a moment before looking back at the short, blonde girl seated at the table. He didn't know what to make of her. He walked over to the door and pulled it open.

Mrs. Coben stood on the other side of the door with a tattered brown purse slung over her shoulder. "Are you done questioning my daughter, detective?"

"Quite done," the young detective answered. "She's free to go."

Patty hadn't wanted to go to the hospital. Her injuries weren't severe enough. She just had a couple of bruises, a cut lip, and some broken skin around her cheekbones. She'd live. She marveled in the mirror, running slender fingers over the welts on her cheeks. Tabatha was so easy to frame. She wasn't even proving to be a challenge, which was quite disappointing.

She turned away from the mirror and headed towards the canopy bed. She hadn't yet had the time, but she really needed to redecorate this room. It was fit for a seven year old girl, not a seventeen year old girl. All of the pink bed garments made her want to hurl.

She sat on the edge of the bed and lifted her backpack from where it leaned against the nightstand. She rummaged through the front pocket, in search of the pamphlet she was given by Aidan at Hidden Treasures. She didn't find it in the large front pocket, so she looked in the main compartment of the backpack. She didn't find it there either.

With furrowed brows, she tossed the backpack on the floor and started digging through the nightstand drawer. There was nothing of importance in the drawer.

She crouched down to the floor and peered beneath the bed, ransacked the dresser drawers, and checked the backpack again. It wasn't possible. There was no way she could have left the pamphlet at school or at Zander's. She never removed it from her backpack, not after she'd snuck into her old bedroom to retrieve it. So if *she* didn't have it, who did?

Her lips pressed tightly together and her eyes narrowed into slits when the obvious answer occurred to her.

Dana, Stephanie, and Mary were concerned about her. That was apparent by the number of voice messages Tabatha had waiting for her when she got home. Mrs. Coben hadn't said a word to her while they were in the car. She hadn't offered advice or expressed concern over the fact that she'd been brought in a second time for questioning in the murder of one of her classmates. Maybe there was something more to Patty's claims that her parents never paid attention to her.

Patty's little brother was spending the night at a friend's house, so she didn't have to worry about him running amuck. Once she was inside the house, she headed straight to her room, where she checked the pamphlet to see if there was another step. There wasn't.

She collapsed into bed, feeling drained of all energy. She dozed off and dreamt about the Homecoming Dance.

The audience had gone crazy after her admission of the prank she and Zander had pulled on Patty Coben. Some of the girls were shaking their head in sympathy. Most of the boys were hooting and hollering with laughter and catcalls. She saw Patty fainting and collapsing on the stage.

Zander had been petrified. He kept asking whether or not Patty was all right. He kept trying to shake her back to consciousness. He was convinced that something was really wrong with her. "She could have a health condition," he'd said. "She could have a health condition we didn't know about, and if she's messed up or hurt somehow, it would be our fault."

Tabatha had rolled her eyes at him. She hadn't bothered kneeling to the floor to see if the other girl was all right. "She'll live," she muttered, flipping her hair over her shoulder.

Zander narrowed his eyes at her. "Can you really be that cold?"

"Like this is news to you?" she tossed at him over her shoulder as she stepped down from the stage.

The chaperones had escorted Patty to the nurse's office, where they let her rest until she woke up.

Tabatha came awake with a start. She wiped at her eyes and realized she'd been crying in her sleep. She had truly been vicious to Patty, and she hadn't felt any remorse over what she'd done until she had *become* Patty Coben. Everything that Zander had called her, everything he'd accused her off, was true. She *had been* cold and heartless. She hadn't cared about anyone other than herself. People catered to her and treated her like a princess, but she'd never done anything to deserve it. People had treated her like that ever since she was a little girl. She'd never known why. She'd assumed it had been because her parents had a lot of money. She was sure some of the high school boys treated her that way because she had good looks.

She hadn't cared enough about the people around her to know their motives. She'd taken advantage of everyone she'd crossed paths with. She'd used people to get what she wanted, and she'd broken a couple of hearts along the way. If she'd been given more time, she would have probably eventually broken Zander's heart.

She swiped the tears away with the backs of her hands and felt around the top of her nightstand for the pamphlet. Her hand brushed against it and she flicked on the lamp.

Sure enough, there was a third step.

Step 3: bind her hair with yours

She grabbed the brush from the nightstand drawer, the one that she'd lifted from Patty's backpack. Then she plucked out a strand of her own hair. She pulled a strand of dark hair from the brush and twisted the blonde hair she'd plucked from her own head with the ebony strand of hair.

On the next blank page, the fourth step had already started to etch itself. A general outline of the words became visible, and then began to darken. The dark ink bled into the paper until she could finally make out the words on the page.

Step 4: light a black candle

Since she didn't have a black candle, it seemed that she'd have to pay Hidden Treasures another visit.

❀❀❀❀❀❀❀❀❀❀❀❀❀❀❀❀❀❀❀❀❀❀❀❀❀❀❀❀❀

chapter nineteen

❀❀❀❀❀❀❀❀❀❀❀❀❀❀❀❀❀❀❀❀❀❀❀❀❀❀❀❀❀

Tabatha decided to walk to the store the next day. She didn't want to have to bother Dana or Mrs. Coben for a ride to the store and it wasn't that far from the Coben residence.

She tucked the pamphlet into the back pocket of her jeans as she entered the store. A bell at the top of the door tinkled as she opened and closed it. Aidan Powers was nowhere in sight. She walked through the narrow aisles of the store and stopped when she reached a door at the back of the shop.

The door was unmarked. It could have been a bathroom, it could have been a back room, or it could have even been a closet. She had no idea where this doorway led. She wondered if she should even open it.

Figuring she wasn't in the position to chicken out at this point, she grabbed the door handle and turned it. She pulled the door open. Darkness greeted her. She ran her hand along the wall, feeling for a light switch. There was none. She entered the room and the door closed silently at her back.

She could hear a man talking, but couldn't make out the words until she drew farther into the room.

Aidan was standing at the center of the room and a series of semi-transparent images hovered over him. The images came together to form a slender blonde woman running away from someone. Tabatha couldn't make out who or what the woman was running from.

"Step two," Aidan was saying. "Embrace your rage." As he spoke, a different image replaced the first. A blonde woman sat up in bed, picked up the pamphlet from where she'd tossed it on the floor, and began to scribble the words that Aidan had uttered.

"Is that how you do it?" Tabatha whispered.

He whirled around and the hologram disappeared. He stepped down from the podium, wearing a heavy velvet robe over his button-down shirt and slacks. Without speaking, he removed the robe and hung it up in a closet at the far end of the room.

"I didn't mean to eavesdrop," she said, sensing his annoyance even from where she stood.

"But you did."

"I was looking for you and you weren't in the store."

"I'm guessing you've reached the fourth step."

She gestured towards where the hologram had been displayed. "Do you even have to ask?"

He rolled his eyes and stepped past her. "Close the door behind you," he ordered.

"So the steps don't create themselves," the teenager mused aloud as she followed him into the main area of the store. "You are the one who tells us what to do. Those are your words in those pamphlets. And the reason the pamphlets are empty at first is because you have us fill them in."

"I can have you fill them in, or I can make the words appear of their own accord," Aidan said vaguely.

"Why don't you just have the steps outlined in the pamphlets when they're in the store if everyone has the same steps?"

"The steps are not always the same," he explained as he walked past a row of jars. He perused the shelves until he found what he was looking for.

"But you told that girl to bind her hair with someone else's hair. I had to do that."

"And Patricia had to do that," he explained, "but not everyone has to do that. I believe this is what you came here for." He held up a black candle.

She couldn't bring herself to let the subject drop, though. All of a sudden, she realized just how much she was trusting Aidan. All of a sudden she wondered whether everything that had happened was her fault or whether or not everything was Aidan's fault.

He set the candle on the shelf and turned to face her. "I don't appreciate the fact that you are trying to blame me for all of the negativity that has come to you.

"You were a cruel, mean girl who had the world at her feet. You took everything in your life for granted. You had everything and yet you were still insecure enough in yourself to make everyone else around you feel miserable. You had a boyfriend who would do anything for you and you used him. You had a family that loved you and you ignored them. You *could* have had friends, but you pushed everyone away from you whenever they tried to get close to you. You crushed a girl's heart without mercy and you wonder why she's become such a hateful, evil monster?"

Tabatha brought a hand up to her throat and took a step back, shocked by the man's frank words. "I didn't mean for all of this to happen," she said.

"It doesn't matter that you didn't mean for it to happen," he said. "It's happening. She is out there killing for the sake of keeping your body. And all because of the fact that you thought you would get a cheap thrill out of humiliating her in front of the entire school."

She couldn't seem to catch her breath.

His eyes sparkled with an unnatural brilliance as he said, "If it were up to me, I would let her keep your body. You think because you cut carbohydrates out of your diet, you deserve to have this wonderful life that has been handed to you. You're wrong.

"The only reason I am going to help you get your body back is because she violated the one rule that I gave her, which was to follow the directions without malice. She has disobeyed me and for that, she will most likely pay with her life. It would be in your best interests not to disobey me."

At first glance, Aidan Powers seemed like a kind, gentle shop owner. It seemed that there was another side to him that most didn't get to see.

He offered the dark candle to her again and said, "My name is Aidan Powers, and I do just that: aid in powers. If you have problems that you need help in conquering, by all means, come to me for help. But if you disobey me, then I cannot protect you from the harm that will come to you.

"The powers that you are invoking are strong, and they are not meant to be used to cause harm to others. Do not use these powers with an intent that is evil in nature. Do not deliberately attempt to cause harm to others."

He didn't charge her anything for the candle and he didn't have to tell her to keep quiet about what she had seen in the back room of the shop. She walked out of the store, feeling extremely disoriented. She couldn't help but wonder just how powerful Aidan was. And what was he? A warlock? A wizard? Something else entirely?

As curious as she was about the elusive shop owner, she didn't have much time to dwell on Aidan Powers. She had to focus on saving Zander from that evil witch Patty and getting her body back.

She headed back to her house and nearly stumbled backwards when she pushed the door to Patty's bedroom open and saw that the room had been picked apart.

She stepped into the room, noting that the bed mattress sat askew on the box spring. The nightstand drawer had been pulled all the way out and appeared to have been thrown across the room. The window curtains had been pulled from their rods. The closet door was open and all of Patty's clothes were piled in a heap in front of the closet.

The old vanity in the corner now had a crack in the mirror, and scribbled across the mirror with red lipstick were the words:

I want my book back and I know you are the one who has it.

—The new, improved *Tabatha*

chapter twenty

"I hear you're throwing a killer Halloween party, man."

Zander closed his locker and came face to face with Brian Grayson. Brian was the star of the school's swim team. "I throw one every year," Zander replied as he started walking in the general direction of his first period class.

"Are there going to be a lot of hot girls there?"

"You doubt me?" Zander returned.

Brian grinned and casually ran a hand through his short, dark hair. "Not that you even have to worry about looking at other girls since you have Tabatha."

"There's no harm in looking," Zander said with a shrug.

They talked for a few more minutes, but eventually Zander ended the conversation and headed for his algebra class. He was more than a little shocked to see Patty Coben standing near the doorway of his first period classroom.

"I have to talk to you," she said.

"This isn't the best time."

"You can skip this class."

"I don't *want* to skip this class," he said.

"You skip this class all the time," she countered. "Would one more time really hurt?"

He slung his backpack over his shoulder, seemingly at a loss for words. It wasn't that he didn't want to skip algebra. There was always some silly excuse he could make up for skipping it. One of the cute brainy girls sitting in the front row would copy her notes for him and even clue him in to some of the answers for that day's homework. He wasn't worried about skipping. He was worried about what Tabatha would do to him if she heard that he'd skipped class to talk to Patty. She'd flip her lid.

She rolled her eyes at him. "Were you always this big of a lapdog?"

He straightened his posture and his eyes spit fire at the insinuation. "I'm not anyone's lapdog," he said.

"You're always following after her and you obey everything she tells you. Sounds like a lapdog to me."

He frowned and grabbed her by the elbow, steering her away from the classroom and into a dark, narrow hallway. "What is it you want from me? Do you want money? Do you want to slap me? What would make you feel better? What would stop you from attacking Tabatha whenever you see her?"

"I don't want anything from you," she told him honestly. "I just want to warn you."

"About?"

"The girl you're calling Tabatha."

His frown deepened.

"She's not really Tabatha."

"She's not? She could have fooled me."

She crossed her arms over her chest. This was going to be a lot more difficult than she thought. "She's not Tabatha," she continued, "because *I'm* Tabatha."

"I don't have time for this, Coben." He made as if to turn and leave.

She reached out and caught his wrist in his hand. He didn't turn around, but he didn't withdraw his wrist from her grasp either. "I'm serious, Zander. I don't know how she managed to do it. But after we played that prank on her, she managed to switch our bodies. And she's been parading around in my car and kissing on *my* boyfriend."

He looked down at her. "You're not Tabatha," he said in a voice laced with concern. "You're Patty Coben. And I'm sorry for what we did to you, but you should seriously seek help." He finally did pull out of her grasp and started walking away from her.

"You have to believe me, Zander!" she shouted. She frantically searched for a fact that only she would know. "When you were eight years old, you lost the only dog you've ever had."

He stopped in his tracks, but didn't stop to face her.

"His name was Connor and I used to always tease you because most people give their dogs names like Sparky and Fluffy and things like that, but you gave your dog a people name. And you always used to say that Connor was…"

"A part of the family," he finished for her.

"You loved him so much, you couldn't even be the one to bury him," she continued. "So your dad had to bury him for you, and you gave him a funeral as if he were really part of the family. You invited all of the kids in the neighborhood to attend the funeral. You had a big picture of Connor near the box that your dad put him in."

"I still have that picture," he said in a distant voice.

"That was when you were eight. When you were ten, your dad wanted to get a new dog, but you wouldn't let him because you said no one would ever replace Connor."

He turned to face her. "How could you possibly know that about me?"

"I know a lot of things about you," she said softly. "You always thought that I never paid attention or listened to you, but I did. I was always listening."

He was shaking his head in disbelief. "But…you can't be Tabatha," he whispered. "It's not possible for people to switch bodies."

"Tell that to Aidan," Tabatha muttered.

"What?"

"Patty went to a store called Hidden Treasures. That's how she was able to do it. It's a magic store."

"But…you can't be her," he repeated.

"I don't want you to focus on that right now. The reason I had to talk to you is because I think Patty wants to hurt you for what we did to her."

"Hurt me?"

"I think she wants to kill you. She is the one who killed Shelly and Ricky. I think you're next."

He laughed outright. "You can't be serious. I mean, *listen* to yourself. This is sounding crazy."

"I know how crazy it sounds, but I couldn't live with myself if I didn't try to warn you about how deranged she is. She's got some kind of weird plan. She ransacked my room, and she's framing me for the murder of Shelly and Ricky."

He ran both of his hands through his hair. "So you pull me aside, you dump all of this on me, and expect me to…what?"

"Be careful," she said before walking around him and leaving him alone in the narrow hallway.

Stephanie wanted to test Patty, so during the lunch period she sat a few tables down from Patty. Just before the lunch bell sounded, Stephanie cupped her hands around her mouth and shouted, "Hey, Patty!"

Patty stopped what she was doing and turned around to see who had called her name.

That night, Zander watched his girlfriend's every move. Not that he was taking Patty Coben seriously. The girl was off of her rocker. He didn't mind taking the blame for it. His prank was most likely the cause of her losing her marbles. Sure, she knew about Connor. But how difficult was it for someone to find out that he used to have a dog that died?

Still, he had noticed that Tabatha had been acting different lately. Well…two weeks ago, she was behaving strangely. She was back to her normal, superficial self nowadays. And he definitely couldn't believe that she'd killed Ricky and Shelly. She wouldn't have had any motive. Shelly was one of her friends and she hadn't known Ricky. Granted, a few of his friends had told him that Ricky had taken Tabatha to the hottest pizza joint in town, but there was no way he could believe that either. His friend had to be mistaken. Why would Tabatha be interested in Ricky when she was dating the most popular boy in school? None of it made sense.

If he believed Patty's story, everything would at least make a little sense. If Tabatha was really Patty, it would explain why she had been acting strangely. It would also explain why she would go to a pizza joint with Ricky. She'd even have motive for the murders of Shelly and Ricky, not to mention the means to get away with them.

"How about this one?" His girlfriend popped out of the dressing room, dressed in a tight, low-cut shirt and a tight skirt.

"You don't think that outfit is showing too much skin?" he asked, his eyebrows knitting together. "If you dropped something, you wouldn't be able to bend over and pick it up."

"If I drop something, you're there to pick it up for me, silly," she said, tossing her hair and smoothing down the skirt. "I like it. I think I'm going to get it."

He shrugged. "I don't even know why you drag me here if you're not going to listen to my opinion."

"For moral support."

He frowned.

"What?" she asked, picking up on his negative mood immediately.

He started to tell her about the encounter that he had with Patty, but thought better of that and merely shook his head. "Nothing. It's just been a hard day."

"We can cut the shopping short if you want," she offered.

He shook his head. He had more observing to do. "Shop until you pass out," he said.

She smiled and disappeared into the dressing room again.

"Babe," he called to her.

"Yeah?" she called back.

"Do you remember the story I told you about Connor?"

There was no response.

"Did you hear me, babe?"

"Yeah," she said, standing on tiptoe so that she could look at him over the top of the dressing room door.

"Well? Do you remember what I told you about him? What happened to him when I was eight?"

"About Connor?" she repeated.

"Yeah."

"He was like...your best friend, right? Back then?"

He nodded, feeling a bit relieved. "Yeah, he was."

"Of course I remember what you told me. He was very important to you."

"He really was."

"Why did you ask me that?" she asked, lowering so that she disappeared out of sight. "Did you bump into him recently?"

A lump formed in Zander's throat. "Did I bump into him?" he repeated.

"Yeah...did you run into him? Is that why you brought him up?"

"Um...no, I didn't run into him," he answered. "He's dead, babe. He died when I was eight."

The dressing room door opened abruptly and she stood there in a t-shirt and her underwear, looking pain-stricken. "How could I forget that? That had to be so tough for you. Did Ricky's funeral remind you of that?"

He hadn't thought of using that as an excuse, but it fit perfectly. He nodded his head.

She walked out of the dressing room and wrapped her arms around him. "Do you keep in touch with his family?"

He scratched his head. "Whose family? Ricky's?"

"No. Connor's."

He gave her the strangest look.

She laughed and backed away from him. "What?"

"Connor was my dog, Tabs."

"Oh. *Right*."

"How could you forget about that?"

She shrugged her shoulders. "I don't know."

"No. I seriously need to know how you could forget about that."

She folded her arms over her chest. "What is your problem?"

An older woman perusing through clearance items eyed the teenage couple warily, most likely noting that the dark-haired girl wasn't dressed in anything but her t-shirt and underwear. She ambled away, giving the couple their privacy.

"I've talked to you a lot about Connor," he said in a steely voice. "It's impossible that you could forget about him like that. I mean...not remembering that he's a dog? You were always getting on my case because I gave him a 'people name' and not a 'dog name.'"

"I'm sorry I forgot, but do I deserve to be yelled at because of it?" she demanded.

He stared at her for a few moments. It was possible for someone to dig up information on his childhood. Could it be possible then for that same person to completely wipe the memory of the person who *should* know about his childhood? It had to be unlikely in this situation.

Which would lead him to believe that Patty Coben was telling the truth...and that would be crazy, right?

His girlfriend - or whoever this girl was - was staring at him with her head tilted to the side. He could only wonder what she was thinking about him.

He didn't get a chance to find out. The cell phone in her purse started chirping. She retrieved her purse from the back of his chair and removed the cell phone from it. She flipped it open and said, "Hello?" She paused for a moment, listening to the person on the other line. "Right now?"

Zander watched the expression on her face closely.

"No, it's not that. It's just that I'm on a date right now. This can't wait until tomorrow?" Another pause as she listened to the response. "I guess I can come in, but it's only a few questions, right? I have to get up early in the morning. Okay. That should be fine. I'll see you in a few minutes, detective."

Zander's ears perked up. Why was a detective calling her?

chapter twenty*one

"I'm so glad you could make it in," Detective Warner greeted in a cheerful voice after offering her a bottle of water.

"What is this about, detective?" Patty asked, standing near his desk. She was wearing the new skirt she'd purchased at Wet Seal and the tight, cerulean blue top. She apparently didn't intend to sit down.

"I just had a few questions for you."

"You interrupted my date for a few questions?"

"A few *important* questions," he corrected.

She heaved a sigh and sat down in the chair. After a moment of thought, she grabbed the bottled water, removed the cap, and took a sip.

"Do you mind if I record this interview?"

She shrugged.

He pressed the Record button on an ancient-looking tape player. "Can you please state your name for me?"

"Pa-" she stopped herself.

His eyes narrowed. "Excuse me?"

She chuckled and flipped her hair. "Tabatha Andrews," she answered.

"And how well did you know Ricky Kellerman?"

"I barely *did* know him."

"I have a couple of sources who state that you were seen at his funeral."

"That is correct."

"And you went to his family's house after the funeral?" the detective pressed.

"Yes, I did."

"Do you often go to the funerals of people you barely know?"

"Zander wanted both of us to go."

"And by Zander, you are referring to your boyfriend, is that correct?"

"Yes."

"Did you go on a date with Ricky on the night he was killed?" the detective asked, watching her face closely.

Her eyes widened. "Why would I go on a date with Ricky?"

He shrugged his shoulders. "I'm not sure. That is why I'm asking."

"I saw Ricky a few times in school and I may have talked to him for awhile. I may have talked with Ricky that night, but I definitely wasn't on a date with him."

"You were involved in an altercation with Patricia Coben on the day of Ricky's funeral. What started that altercation?"

"Patty Coben is a psychopath," the slender teenager said without hesitation. "Zander and I played a prank on her and she still hasn't gotten past it. It's not the first time she has attacked me."

"I do remember that, yes. And it looks like she punched you pretty badly. You tried to cover up the bruises with makeup, but I can still see them."

"Gee, thanks, detective," she said, giving him her sweetest smile.

He shrugged again. "So you didn't have any reason to want to cause harm to Ricky Kellerman?"

"Are you serious?" she asked him. "Is that why you pulled me in here? You think I could have had something to do with it?"

"We're simply following all of the leads we have at this point," he explained. "I don't want you to take any offense. I have to ask these questions. We want to get to the bottom of this."

"You could start off by talking to the person who actually killed Shelly and Ricky."

"And who would that be?" the detective asked.

The dark-haired girl lowered her head and positioned her lips close to the microphone of the tape recorder. "Patty Coben," she replied. "Patty Coben is the one who killed Shelly and Ricky."

Tabatha lit the black candle with the pamphlet lying on the floor, open to a blank page. The only light in the room besides the light of the candle was the moonlight streaming in from the window. She wondered if Aidan was watching her right now. Could he see what she was doing? Was he preparing to fill in the fifth step, or would he wait until she went to sleep?

Before she could get an answer to her rhetorical question, a light tap sounded at the window. She stood on her feet and walked over to the window. She peered down and into the backyard of the Coben family's house. A dark silhouette was standing beneath her window.

A tiny gasp escaped her lips. She couldn't tell who it was from where she stood. Would she be endangering herself by going downstairs to get a closer look?

She let the curtain fall back into place and exited her room. She walked down the hall, nearly tripped down the stairs, and into the kitchen. The kitchen was located right below her bedroom. Once in the kitchen, she walked over to the back door and peered out of the glass panel. All she could see was her own reflection staring at her.

She unlocked the door and twisted the knob. Her heart was pounding beneath her chest as she stepped out onto the back porch. The night breeze caused the maple tree leaves to rustle, and she could hear the distinct sound of crickets chirping. There was also something else...was it the sound of someone whispering?

"Over here," she heard someone say.

Her eyes widened and she turned towards the wooded area that closed off the Cobens' backyard.

"Over here," the person said again.

"I'm not going over there," she said in a shaky voice. "You come over here."

There was a pause and the air grew tense. Neither party moved an inch for several minutes. Then, someone emerged from the foliage lining the backyard. That someone had dark, shoulder-length hair pulled back into a ponytail. He was dressed in a plain t-shirt and jeans with holes carved into the knees.

She openly stared at him and he returned the look of perusal. She wanted to run and throw her arms around him. She wanted to launch herself into his arms and kiss him, but most likely she would freak him out if she did either of those things. Instead of attempting to do either of those things, she simply stood on the porch and waited for him to approach her.

He took his time in walking up to her. He had an expression on his face that clearly stated that he didn't know what he was doing here. He spoke anyway. "She didn't know about Connor."

She nodded her head as if she'd figured as much. "I'm not sure how she could possibly know about that."

"She should know, because she's my girlfriend."

"But she's *not* your girlfriend, Zander," she insisted.

"*You* are," he muttered sarcastically.

She shrugged her shoulders and stared down at the ground. "The old me would have rather died than to let you see me in the body of Patty Coben," she said softly. "The old me would have killed myself the very first day I found out I looked anything *like* Patty. I was a superficial wreck. I was a drop-dead gorgeous wreck. But I was still very messed up. And very cruel to everyone around me, including you."

Instead of responding to what she said, he suddenly asked her, "When is my birthday?"

"February thirteenth," she answered automatically.

"And what college am I going to?"

"Arizona State."

"And why?"

"Because they throw killer parties at Arizona State."

He frowned. "Awhile ago, I told Tabatha and only Tabatha what I want to be when I get out of college."

"I was trying to convince you to go into the professional football league," she remembered aloud, closing her eyes. "I thought you were a talented player and I wanted you to have the high profile life of a professional ball player. You told me that you wanted to be a lawyer instead, which confused me."

A pained expression appeared on his face.

"I want you to know that it didn't surprise me because I didn't think you were smart enough. You're extremely smart and you're definitely talented enough to do whatever you want to do, Zander. It just surprised me because in all of the time we'd been together, you'd never brought it up before. All you talked about was football, and then out of the blue you come at me with the lawyer stuff."

He covered his mouth with one of his hands and shook his head. "You're really her," he said, sounding amazed. He turned his back to her and closed his eyes. "Oh my God. If you're her, then I've been dating..."

"Patty Coben," she supplied for him.

"Can you guys switch back? How does all of that work?"

"Supposedly, there is supposed to be a way for us to switch back and I'm working on it." She stepped down from the porch and stood at his back.

He turned around to face her. There were tears in his eyes. "I'm sorry I didn't believe you before."

"It's okay. It's pretty hard to believe."

"And you seem so...different."

"I seem less like a spoiled snob?" she asked with a smile.

He smiled back, nodding his head. "Yeah."

She playfully punched him in the arm.

He rubbed the spot that she'd punched and asked in a more serious tone, "Wait until I see her again. I'm going to let her have it."

"No," she told him. "You can't."

His brows furrowed. "Why can't I? Look at what she did to you. I mean, we hurt her pretty bad with what we did to her on the night of the Homecoming Dance, but she's out there *killing* people, right? We've got to confront her. We've got to confront her and turn her in before she gets to someone else."

"We can't, not yet," she argued.

"So what am I supposed to do? Continue dating her?" he joked.

"That's exactly what you're supposed to do," she confirmed.

He was already shaking his head before she could get the entire sentence out. "I refuse to do that, Tabs. I'm sorry. I can't continue hanging out with her, knowing who she is and what she's done."

"You have to. Right now, it's her word against ours."

"Meaning?"

"Meaning we have to get some hardcore evidence before confronting her," she replied readily. "And since you're dating her, you're just the person to get it."

His lips pursed into a thin line.

She asked in a cheerful voice, "You want to be a lawyer, right? You should know how importance evidence is in a situation like this."

He shrugged his shoulders in defeat. "Fine. I'll do it."

She smiled prettily at him. "I know."

He brought a hand up and touched her cheek lightly. It was strange. The face wasn't Tabatha's, the body wasn't Tabatha's, and the voice wasn't Tabatha's. And yet, Tabatha's aura seemed to dominate the space that they were standing in. She was, without a doubt, his girlfriend. He brushed the wayward blonde hair back from her face and lowered his head so that he could press a gentle kiss to her lips.

The kiss was short, but it was enough to bring tears to her eyes. She lowered her head, too ashamed to look at him.

"I don't want you to worry," he said to her. "Everything is going to be all right."

"What if everything isn't all right, though?" she asked him. "What if I have to live the rest of my life in Patty's body?"

"Then we'll make the best of the situation."

"I wouldn't be the pretty cheerleader anymore, though."

"I never cared about that, Tabs," he said sternly. "You cared about all of that stuff way more than I did. I'm in love with you. You'll always be beautiful to me."

The tears really came then, and her knees nearly buckled when his arms circled around her.

chapter twenty•two

On Tuesday morning, Patty walked through the school doors wearing her flashiest stiletto heels, tightest blouse, and the shortest skirt that she could get away with while on campus. Her slender tanned legs were enough to make the male student body stop whatever they were doing and give her their full attention. Whistles sounded immediately. She didn't acknowledge any of the classmates who greeted her.

She walked straight to Tabatha's locker, where Zander was waiting for her. She smiled at the mere sight of him. For some reason, she felt that he might not show up this morning. She didn't know why a thought like that would occur to her. In this instance, she was glad that she was proven wrong.

He greeted her with a hug and offered to hold her backpack for her. "Have you gotten your Halloween costume yet?" he asked her.

She twisted the dial on the locker and pulled it open. The previous week, she'd gotten another combination from the school office. She'd claimed to have forgotten her original locker combination. "My Halloween costume?" she repeated, sounding deep in thought.

"Yeah. For my party this weekend."

"I almost forgot about the party. I don't have my costume yet, but I will."

"You're a serial procrastinator," he accused lightly.

She arched a look at him over her shoulder and smiled. "But you love it," she said knowingly as she grabbed a couple of textbooks from her locker. She stood on tiptoe so that she could give him a kiss.

149

He pulled back at first, giving her a strange look.

She narrowed her eyes at him. "Do I have food stuck in my teeth or something?"

He shook his head. "No. I haven't brushed my teeth this morning. I just didn't want to gross you out."

"Don't be silly. I want a kiss before I go to first period."

He obliged her with a quick kiss on the lips. He didn't kiss her a millisecond longer than he had to, though. As soon as he felt that it was safe to pull back from the kiss, he did.

"You're really acting weird today, Zander," she said.

"I'm just on edge, that's all."

"Where did you go last night after I had to leave?"

"I just hung out with Brian and Freddy for awhile," he lied. "Where did you go?"

She shrugged her shoulders without speaking.

"The guy who called you on your phone, you called him a detective."

"They wanted to ask me a couple of questions about Ricky at the police station."

He looked surprised. "Why would they want to ask you anything about him? You didn't know Ricky that well, right?"

"Who knows what the cops are thinking," she muttered.

"What kind of questions did they ask you?"

"Stupid ones."

"What did you tell them?"

"I told them what I could. I told them that I didn't know Ricky that well, but that I knew who killed him."

Zander's brows knit together. "You do?"

"Everyone does," she said simply. "It was Patty Coben. She's gone totally bonkers and she keeps jumping on me every chance she gets."

"And you told the cops that?"

She nodded her head vigorously. "I'm going to be late to first period, babe. I have to get going. I'll try to get my Halloween costume today after school. I'll see you at lunch?"

He nodded his head, but he was already deep in thought about the information she'd just given him.

"Are you losing weight?" Mary asked during lunch period.

Tabatha looked down at herself. She couldn't really tell, not in this body. "I don't know."

"I think you are," Dana said.

"Lucky me," Tabatha mumbled.

Dana laughed. "Is it that bad, being Patty Coben?"

"Only when she's being framed for murder," Tabatha responded. "Everyone in school has been avoiding me like the plague. The ones who make fun of me are even worse now. They all seriously think that I killed Ricky and Shelly."

"It has to be tough," Stephanie said.

"I can't imagine having to live through it," Mary agreed. "It takes a strong person to be able to go through all of this without going nuts."

"I second that notion," Dana chimed in.

Tabatha shrugged. She'd already clued them into the fact that Zander believed that she was the real Tabatha and that Patty was evil. They'd been shocked to discover that, but they definitely took it as a good sign.

That morning when she'd looked at the pamphlet, there hadn't been another step outlined on the next blank page. The black candle was just a dried puddle of wax by that time, so she couldn't have lit it again if she'd wanted to. She didn't know what she was supposed to do next. Without the guidance of the pamphlet, she was helpless. And that is why she took the pamphlet wherever she went, especially after seeing that her room had been ransacked by Patty.

"What we need to do is come up with a plan," Dana was saying.

"We should carry out the plan at the Halloween party that Zander is throwing," Mary said excitedly. "It would be the perfect time."

"I don't even know what I'm going to dress up as," Stephanie said with a pensive expression on her face.

"I doubt we'll be invited," Dana said.

"I know what I'm going as," Tabatha said suddenly.

Her three friends all turned to look at her. They were waiting for her to clue them in to what her costume was going to be, but she didn't supply them with any more information. "Well?" Dana prompted.

"I'm going to go as Tabatha Andrews."

Dana coughed. Stephanie blinked. Mary fidgeted.

"It's the perfect costume, really."

"But..." Stephanie started.

"You look nothing like her," Dana finished.

"I know. But I will." Tabatha smiled and stood from the table.

"Is this your car?"

Patty halted in her steps at the sight of Detective Warner leaning against her car. "It's you...again."

"I just had a few more questions for you," he called to her, squinting his eyes against the sun's blinding rays. "I was hoping you had a minute."

"For you, detective, always," she said sarcastically. "It's not like I really have a choice, right?"

"This is true."

"What questions did you have for me?"

"I don't want to talk here. Is there somewhere we can go where there aren't crazed noisy teenagers running around like preschoolers on a sugar high?"

"We have a courtyard. There probably isn't anyone there now."

"Lead me to it." In the process of following her, he was nearly mowed down by a sophomore on his ten-speed. "As soon as the bell rings, you guys all pretty much stampede your way out of the building, don't you?"

"I don't know how it was when you were a teenager, but not many of us actually like going to school," she told him.

"My teenage years weren't that long ago," he muttered as he followed her around the school building.

She stopped at a glass door and tested the handle. "They haven't locked the doors yet," she informed him. "We're in luck."

He followed her through the door and closed the door behind him. They were now in the school's courtyard. There were benches, tables, trees, and small hills of well-manicured green grass. If they wanted, they could continue walking through another set of glass doors and they would be in the school's cafeteria.

Content with the location she'd chosen, he claimed a seat on one of the benches. She remained standing with her arms folded across her chest.

His eyes traveled from the tips of her pink stilettos, up the length of her legs and to the matching pink top she wore. "The school dress code has changed since I went to high school."

She smirked at him in response. "What are your questions?"

He withdrew a small notepad from his jacket pocket. "Right. I just wanted to clarify a few things to make sure I understood you clearly. You didn't know Ricky Kellerman that well. You did state that the night he was killed, you weren't on a date with him. Is that right?"

"I told you once, detective. I didn't go out on a date with Ricky Kellerman. How many times do I have to tell you that?"

"I'm not sure how many times you have to tell me that before I believe it," he said, "because your fingerprints were located in the Kellermans' house. As a matter of fact, they were located in the same room that Ricky was attacked in."

chapter twenty·three

Patty blinked her eyes rapidly. She couldn't have heard the detective correctly. "Excuse me?"

He grinned at her. "Your fingerprints were at the scene."

"How would you even know what my fingerprints look like?" she managed to croak when she finally found her voice.

"The water bottle that I offered you last night," he answered easily. "I didn't throw it away. I had the lab run some tests on it to identify the fingerprints you left on it. And then I had those fingerprints compared to the ones found at the scene that didn't belong to the Kellerman family."

"Well, I...I went to the funeral," she stammered. "And afterwards, I went to the Kellerman house. The gathering was held in the living room. I could have left my fingerprints then."

He stood from the bench, lightly tapping the pencil on the surface of the notepad. "We lifted the fingerprints from the scene on the night of the murder," he told her. "Nice try."

She backed away from him, looking frightened. "I don't understand," she said. "Patty is the one who killed Ricky and Shelly. Not me."

"You weren't honest with me about how well you knew Ricky," the detective went on as if he hadn't heard her. "That kind of makes me wonder what else you weren't honest about."

"This can't be legal," she whispered. "The water bottle and coming to my school like this...none of this can be legal."

"I offered you the water. You didn't throw it away. You just left it on my desk. And when I came to your school, you offered to show me to the courtyard so I could ask you my questions."

She lifted her chin a notch. "It's your word against mine," she said.

He laughed. "And what is that supposed to mean? Are you trying to threaten me?"

She closed the short distance between them and rose on her tiptoes. She looked as if she were about to kiss him, but instead she whispered into his ear, "You don't know how dangerous I can be."

He whispered back, "Quite the contrary, my dear. I think I know *just* how dangerous you can be."

"What is stopping me from going to your boss and telling him that you harassed me?" she asked him.

He looked confused. "What?"

She brushed her lips against his cheek and pressed a kiss to his lips. He resisted her and pulled back, looking stunned. "Don't you find me attractive?" she asked, pouting prettily at him. She turned around in a small circle, glancing at him over her shoulder.

He took a step back from her, but she moved with him and unexpectedly reached out and scratched his forearm.

Waving her fingers at him, she said, "Now I have your skin underneath my fingernails. I've watched enough reruns of *Law and Order* to know how incriminating that is."

"You're crazy," he said under his breath.

"I'm worse." She kissed him again, satisfied when he didn't resist her this time.

When the kiss started to heat up a little too quickly for her comfort, she pushed him away from her and wiped her mouth with the back of her hand. "Hold on, cowboy," she said breathlessly.

A wild look had come into his eyes, and now it settled.

"I don't want you to go getting into trouble on my account," she continued. "Anyone can barge in on us here."

"What are you suggesting?" he asked carefully.

"I suggest that we move this to a place where we can have more privacy."

A wolfish smile appeared on his face.

She drove and ordered him to follow her. She led him to Lookout Point. Not many teenagers drove to Lookout Point anymore, and even if they did, chances were that it wouldn't be during daylight hours. When she pulled her car up to Lookout Point, there was no one in sight. That was just the way she wanted it.

The detective parked his unmarked car next to hers and immediately stepped out of the car. He stretched his arms over his head as if he had been driving for the past five hours, not just the past five minutes. "Nice spot," he called out to her.

She shrugged. "I like to come here and think sometimes," she lied smoothly, walking up to him. "I figured no one would be here during the day, so we'd have the place to ourselves."

"Good thinking," he said, and didn't hesitate to kiss her.

She flirtatiously dodged his kisses and waved an index finger at him. "I have a few questions for you first."

"So you're going to interrogate *me* now?" he said, laughing.

"What made you think to lift my prints by offering me a water bottle?"

His expression sobered. "I can't tell you the answer to that."

"Yes you can," she said, pressing a kiss to his cheek and running her hand through his hair.

"No, I can't," he insisted.

She pouted. "Well, that's disappointing."

He laughed and pressed his forehead to hers. "I can think of a lot more fun things we could be doing instead of interrogating each other."

"And I'm sure we'll get to those fun things, but first I want my questions answered," she told him.

He straightened and narrowed his eyes at her. "What is this?"

"What is what?"

He gestured around him. *"This.* You didn't bring me here because you wanted privacy, did you?"

"You're such a good little detective," she said silkily, pressing herself against him and kissing him. Her arms slid around his waist in a tight embrace. One of her hands brushed against a bulky piece of metal.

He greedily kissed her back. "You're so beautiful," he said against her lips.

"I know," she told him as she withdrew the heavy piece of metal from his waistband.

His fingers slid beneath her shirt just as there was a sharp, distinct clicking sound near his right temple. He broke the kiss off and peered down at her.

She was holding his own gun to his head.

"What are you doing?" he asked, even though he already knew the answer to that question.

"I'm holding a gun to your head," she answered matter-of-factly. "Answer my question."

"What..." He pinched the bridge of his nose.

"How did you know to compare my prints to the prints left at the scene? How did you know I was the one who killed Ricky?"

He blinked slowly. "You really *are* her, aren't you?"

She waved the gun at him. "I really am who?"

"Patricia Coben."

She froze. She stopped waving the gun in midair. He knew. He knew who she was. The only way he could know that information was if Patty had told him. In his own way, he had answered her question, so she no longer needed him around. She took a few steps back, gripped the gun in both hands, lined it up with his brow, and pulled the trigger.

He toppled like a Jenga puzzle piece. His face was a bloody, unrecognizable mass. There was a gaping hole and bloody tissue where one of his eyes should have been. She wrinkled her nose in disgust, but aimed the gun at his heart and pulled the trigger again. Just to be sure.

The bell over the door jingled, indicating that someone was entering the store. Aidan sat behind the front counter, reading a heavy spell book with a red velvet cover. He didn't bat an eyelash at the sound of the bell. He didn't blink when a teenage boy came into view, browsing through the items on the shelves. The boy had shoulder-length brown hair and was dressed in a plain t-shirt and a worn pair of jeans.

Even though the store owner didn't budge, he did notice that the boy's nose was wrinkled in disgust. Coupled with that disgust was a twinkle of curiosity in the boy's eyes. People couldn't help but be interested in the wares that Hidden Treasures offered, especially the citizens of this boring, suburban town.

Aidan pushed aside the large book and crossed his arms over his chest, staring unabashedly at the boy. "So I'm going to guess that you're the love interest," he said. His voice echoed in the small shop, bouncing off of the walls.

The boy turned around slowly. "I don't follow."

"You're the boy who was dating Tabatha," the androgynous store owner said, sliding from behind the counter. "And you're the boy who is now dating Patty."

The astonished look on the boy's face was priceless.

"I was beginning to wonder if you were ever going to show up," Aidan continued.

"How do you know who I am?" the boy asked. "And how did you know I'd show up at all?"

The shop owner started to walk idly through the shop, letting his fingers trail along the polished pine shelves. His platinum blonde hair was pulled back from his youthful face and held fast by a simple dark ribbon. He was certain that the clueless teenager would follow him, so he continued to speak in a rich, deep voice. "I know a great deal about you and your situation. You and your girlfriend have created a monster, quite literally, in Patty. She was a happy, carefree girl until you and Tabatha came along with your cruel practical joke." When he didn't hear a response, he turned and arched an eyebrow at the blushing teenage boy.

"We didn't think that anything like this would happen," the boy insisted, stuffing his hands into the front pockets of his jeans.

"No one ever thinks that something like this would happen," Aidan said wisely. He turned his back on the boy and continued down the aisle. "Not many people could foresee events as strange as these."

"How do we stop her?"

"I'm not sure that you can."

"You're kidding, right?"

"The outcome of their encounter is not necessarily predetermined," Aidan said.

Zander snorted. "That's hard to believe, since you seem to know everything."

The graceful store owner arched a glance at the boy over his shoulder. "If Tabatha is doomed to remain in the body of Patty Coben, how would you react?"

"I would be there for her," the boy quickly responded.

"You answered that question without hesitation," Aidan said, allowing his long, tapered fingers to caress a jar filled with sparkling powder. "You would stand beside her, even though she would no longer be the most popular girl in school...the most *beautiful* girl in school?"

"I would stick by her no matter what."

Aidan stopped walking and clasped his hands together in front of him. "I can't promise that you and your girlfriend will come out the victors in this battle. Both sides of this battle are tainted. You and Tabatha were heartless in how you treated other people. It's particularly sad because you are not cruel by nature, but took part in cruel acts for the sake of your girlfriend's amusement. And because of that,

Patty is now no longer a nice, fun-loving girl. She is now a vicious creature who is terrorizing this town."

"You're so quick to blame Tabatha and me," Zander said slowly. "I find it interesting that you don't hold yourself at least partially accountable for everything that's going on. She wouldn't have been capable of something this evil if you hadn't given her that book."

Aidan held up a solitary index finger. "And that is where you are wrong," he said quietly. "If you and Tabatha are to have even the slightest chance against Patty, you need to realize that she didn't need me to create all of this madness. It doesn't matter which body she is contained in. She is capable of a lot more than you're giving her credit for."

The bell over the door chimed. "Aidan, are you here?" a young, feminine voice called.

Zander froze. The voice sounded just like Tabatha's. He wordlessly stared at the shop owner, who casually gave his shoulder a pat before disappearing and greeting his loyal customer.

"What brings you here?" Zander could hear the shop owner asking Patty.

Zander crouched low and listened to the conversation.

"I have a problem," Patty said, sounding extremely anxious. "My pamphlet is missing. I need another one."

"Your pamphlet is missing?" Aidan asked. He did a good job of managing to sound surprised.

"Yeah, and I don't think I'm going to be able to get it back."

Aidan clucked his tongue.

Zander risked a peek around the closest shelf. He could clearly see a girl who looked a lot like his girlfriend. He knew better now, though. He knew that the tall, slender girl he was looking at wasn't his girlfriend. She was someone else-some*thing* else-entirely.

The dark-haired girl twirled a strand of her hair around her finger. "Please tell me you have another pamphlet for me," she begged persistently.

160

Aidan was positioning himself behind the counter. "I'm sorry to tell you that there is no replacement for that pamphlet."

She groaned in frustration.

"Do you have any idea of where the pamphlet could be?"

"I have a *very* good idea of where it is," she said between clenched teeth. Her fists were balled at her sides. She looked as if she were going to spontaneously combust at any moment. "I think that Tabatha has it."

Zander drew in a sharp breath at the mention of Tabatha's name.

"And you're saying that I could risk everything I've worked so hard for if I don't get the book back," she said aloud to herself. "So then, I have to get the pamphlet back, at all costs, right?"

Aidan held up a hand. "I didn't say-" he started.

She bobbed her head up and down. "You're right, of course," she said, already backing up towards the entrance to the store. "I've taken everything else from her, right? How hard could it be to get back a tiny little pamphlet from her?" She disappeared out of the store and the only thing that indicated the entire scene wasn't imagined was a lone tinkling of a gold bell positioned above the magic shop's door.

Brian Grayson and Freddy Schreiber were playfully threatening to throw a cheerleader down the escalator of the town's only mall. They were loud and rowdy and didn't care who heard them. Patty didn't recognize the cheerleader they were hanging out with. All of the cheerleaders looked the same to her.

She *did* recognize Brian and Freddy, though. Zander hung out with them a lot and they both hit on her several times a day. When they saw her, they left the cheerleader alone and trailed her all over the mall as she searched for a Halloween costume.

Brian in particular couldn't seem to keep his hands off of her. He was always reaching for her hand or draping his arm across her shoulders. Whenever he opened one of the department store doors for her, his hand would rest at her lower back. He was extremely bold to hit on his friend's girlfriend, but he didn't seem to care.

Freddy tagged along, seeming to be content with being the third wheel.

Patty tried on costumes and asked for their opinions. They weren't tough critics at all; they loved her in everything, which made her decision all the more difficult.

At some point during the night, she asked Brian, "So what kind of trouble did you and Zander get into last night?"

They were seated in the food court. Brian and Freddy had gotten into a French fry fight, and the bench and table were littered with fried strings of potatoes. Freddy plucked a fry from his curly red hair as he asked, "Last night? What do you mean?"

"You guys all hung out, right?" she asked, taking a sip of her cola. "What kind of trouble did you get into?"

Freddy and Brian exchanged dubious glances. "We didn't hang out with Zander last night," Brian answered finally. "We called him and asked him to hang out, but he said that he was busy."

She frowned. Earlier that day, Zander had told her that after their date last night, he'd spent time with Freddy and Brian. Now, Freddy and Brian were telling her another story. And that would mean that Zander had lied to her. Which begged the question, why would he lie to her?

Seeing another opportunity to hit on her, Brian scooted closer to her. "If he's cheating on you, you can definitely count on me to be there for you," he vowed. "I'm a better boyfriend than he is anyway. I wouldn't even let you out of my sight. I mean, where *is* he, anyway?"

Good question, she thought to herself. Her eyes darkened with malice. Tabatha had run to Detective Warner and she'd told him everything that had happened. She could have just as easily approached Zander. She suddenly stood up and excused herself from the table, not noticing the disappointed expression on Brian's face.

As she strode away from them, Brian leaned across the table and asked his best friend, "What was it? Did I come on too strong?"

Aidan was in his special room, wearing a long robe that pooled around his feet. A series of images hovered in front of him, but he focused on Patty. He watched as she slammed her way into her bedroom and knelt beside the canopy bed. She reached under the bed and pulled out a large book that seemed almost too heavy for her to lift. She dropped it on the bed and began flipping through the pages.

The mysterious store owner made gesturing movements with his hands and zoomed in on the book. He tilted his head to the side and said aloud to no one in particular, "Hmm. That book isn't one of the books that I carry in my store. I wonder where she got that." Then, he continued to watch her, curious as to what she would do next.

chapter twenty·four

Patty watched Zander closely for the next few days. She noticed several subtle changes in his demeanor. He usually couldn't keep his hands off of her, but over the next few days, he was the perfect gentleman. He was never closer to her than he had to be. If they were sitting on the couch together in his family's living room, she sat on one end and he sat on the opposite end of the couch. He didn't kiss her more than he had to. He didn't even attempt to kiss her; she was always the one making the first move when it came to that. He didn't call her as much as he used to, and on Wednesday morning, he failed to meet her at her locker as he usually did. There was definitely something up with him.

Thursday evening, they were sitting on her bed in her bedroom. She had excused herself from the room so she could go to the bathroom. When she returned from the bathroom, she found Zander kneeling on the floor. He was reaching for something underneath her bed.

Frowning, she cleared her throat loudly and came to stand behind him.

He glanced over his shoulder. His face turned beet red as he stood to his feet.

"What were you doing just now?" she asked him.

It didn't take long for him to come up with an answer. "I dropped my keys," he replied. "I was looking for them."

Her eyes were cold and relentless as they searched his face. "Did you find them?"

"No, but there's a big book under your bed. Is that your diary?"

The hair prickled along her forearms. "No, that's not my diary," she snapped. "It's a book that I checked out from the library. I'm using it for research for a history class."

"Oh." He rubbed at the back of his neck.

She narrowed her eyes at him. "You didn't really drop your keys, did you? You were snooping around my room."

He moved away from her and went to stand at the window. "I wasn't snooping around your room," he muttered.

"And I bumped into Brian and Freddy when I was shopping for my Halloween costume," she went on furiously. "You told me that you hung out with them a few days ago, but they told me otherwise."

His back went rigid.

"Where were you, Zander?"

He shrugged his shoulders.

"Are you cheating on me?" she demanded. "Why can't you be honest with me?"

"I'm not cheating on you," he said in a stony voice. "I'd never do that to you."

"I'm not so sure of that," she said snottily. "You're lying to me, you're snooping on me, and lately you've been acting weird."

He sighed and turned to face her. He approached her and collected her in his arms. "I'm sorry, babe," he apologized. "I've just been very stressed out lately. I didn't want to bring you down with all of the things I'm going through right now."

"That's what I'm here for, though," she told him. "If you're having a hard week, you should talk to me about it instead of leaving me in the dark."

He pressed a kiss to her forehead. "I know. I'm sorry."

She felt his arms around her and she felt his soft lips against her forehead, but she didn't know if she believed the story that he was giving her. If he was having a hard week that would explain why he was being a little distant, but it didn't explain why he would be snooping around her room.

So when he left her house that night, she didn't return to her room. She ran outside, hopped into her car, and followed him.

Tabatha sat on the front steps of the Coben family's porch with her arms wrapped around her knees. She perked up when she saw a familiar set of headlights cruising down the street of her neighborhood. Zander's red sports car pulled into her driveway and a moment later, he stood out of the car.

She resisted the urge to run to him and throw her arms around him. Instead, she waited for him to make his way to the porch. Then, she wiped her hands off on her jeans and stood up.

"I snooped around her room and the only thing I found was a big magic book that she hides underneath her bed," he reported shortly after hugging her. "She caught me snooping and got pretty heated about it."

"You have to be careful," she warned.

"I know."

"But she has a magic book under her bed?"

He nodded, running a hand through his hair. "It's huge. She said that she checked it out from the library to use for her history class, but given the circumstances, she's probably lying."

"Yeah."

"I was going to bring the book with me, but I left it there since she caught me."

She hugged him again and happily breathed in the scent of his hair. "That's okay."

"Are you coming to my Halloween party this weekend?" he asked all of a sudden.

"Are you sure you want me there?" she questioned. "I don't think I'd fit in with your friends."

He pulled out of the embrace and rolled his eyes. "I don't care about that. I want you there."

She shrugged her shoulders.

"Have you gotten your costume yet?"

"Not yet. I know what I'm going to dress up as, though."

"What are you going to dress up as?"

She smiled teasingly at him. "I'm not going to tell you. You're going to have to wait and see."

They sat on the porch together and looked up at the stars. They talked until well past midnight even though they had school the next day. They talked and hugged and kissed, and all the while, unbeknownst to them, a pair of evil eyes was locked on them until the moment Zander drove away in his sleek sports car.

After school on Friday night, Tabatha went shopping for her Halloween costume. The mall was packed with people, and she was certain that a lot of them were also shopping for costumes. She was thankful that her costume wasn't extremely complicated. Her entire shopping excursion lasted for a little over an hour, and most of that time was spent standing in line at the department store counter.

When she made it home, she ate dinner with the Coben family. On this particular night, Brendon seemed to have a lot to say. Mr. and Mrs. Coben were also more talkative than usual. They asked Tabatha how her day at school was and asked if she had any plans for Saturday night. She explained that there was a party she was going to.

After dinner, she went upstairs and into Patty's room. She closed the door at her back and set her shopping bags on the floor. She turned on the television that was perched on the dresser. She half-listened to the news while rummaging through the department store bags. She tried the clothing items on while looking in the mirror, and was about to remove the outfit when she heard a familiar name.

She turned her attention on the television. A picture of a detective flashed on the screen as the monotonous voice of the news reporter droned on, "...Body was found last night at the location endearingly called Lookout Point. The department is tight-lipped about the details of this incident. All we know at this point is that the detective was shot at close range and there are currently no suspects in custody. Detective Warner has served with the department for seven years and leaves behind a wife and a daughter..."

Tabatha's mouth dropped open and she dropped onto the bed with wide eyes. Detective Warner was dead. He'd been killed. He was the one person who could have helped her escape the blame for Shelly's and Ricky's murders, and now he was gone. There was no way he could help her now. She was on her own.

She slowly removed the outfit and stood in the mirror in her undergarments, staring at her body. She was definitely losing a lot of weight. Her stomach looked flatter and her arms were more slender than they had been before. After a few more minutes of admiring her new body, she put on some pajamas and stared for a long time at the open pamphlet lying on the nightstand.

Zander had interrupted her as she was obeying Step 4, but the candle had burned throughout the time they'd spent together. When she'd returned to her room that night, the next page had still been blank, but now a fifth step had scribbled itself across the thin, white paper.

Step 5: sleep

Detective Jack Goldenstein went through his deceased partner's desk with a determined look in his dark brown eyes. His dark hair was slicked back from his face and he'd removed his suit jacket and loosened his tie prior to beginning the search for clues. Before he'd been killed, his partner had told him that he was onto something. Goldenstein had thought that the entire case was open-and-shut. The chubby girl, Patty Coben, was obviously the killer. She had the motive and the opportunity. Shelly had made fun of her in front of their classmates. Ricky had dumped her. It didn't take a dummy to put two and two together, but apparently Warner had thought there was something more to the case.

Warner had notes scribbled on every piece of paper that was visible. He had kept two notebooks: one that he kept on him at all times and one that he kept in his desk. The small notepad that had been stashed in his desk drawer held a bunch of random notes written by Warner. On one page, he had scribbled, "Coben girl = innocent." On another page, he'd written, "Coben girl points the finger at T. Andrews." There were notes referencing the fingerprints at the scene of the Kellerman murder. The prints had belonged to Tabatha Andrews.

Jack locked himself in an interrogation room and listened to the Coben and Andrews interviews at length. He listened to the interview with Tabatha first. He wrote down a few notes of his own. Then, he listened to the interview with Patty. His brows furrowed at the topics discussed in the Coben interview.

After the tape clicked, signaling that it was the end of the recording, Jack Goldenstein sat back in his chair, deep in thought.

chapter twenty·five

When Tabatha woke up, she expected to be in her own room, in her own family's house. After all, she'd done everything the pamphlet had told her to do. She was disappointed to discover that she was still in Patty Coben's body.

The phone on the nightstand rang and she reached over to grab it. It was Dana, wanting to know whether or not she needed any help getting her Halloween costume together. Tabatha had told Dana, Mary, and Stephanie about the fact that she'd be attending Zander's Halloween party. She'd even invited them, but they hadn't wanted to attend. They had wished her luck, though.

She talked to Dana for a few minutes, then hung up the phone. The phone rang again. Laughing, she answered the phone. "I don't need help getting my costume together, Dana. I should be fine."

"That's good to hear," said an unfamiliar, deep voice.

She frowned. "Were you calling for my parents?" she asked hesitantly.

"Well, according to you, they're not really your parents, are they?" the voice asked.

Her eyes narrowed. "Is this Aidan?"

"My name is Jack Goldenstein. Detective Warner was my partner, and I've taken it upon myself to catch up on the Woods and Kellerman case. Your name comes up quite often in this case."

"There are people who believe I was the one behind the murders of Shelly and Ricky," she said. "Detective Warner was one of the only people who believed I was innocent."

"And now he's dead," the man on the other end of the line said in an angry voice.

"I was definitely sorry to hear about that," she said quietly.

"Were you?"

She slowly stood up from her bed. Her grip tightened on the phone. "What are you trying to say?"

"That it's possible that he could have discovered something that made him believe that you were guilty of the murders."

"You can't be serious," she said. "You can't believe that I would kill Detective Warner."

"I don't know what to believe. You tell this tall tale in the interview with my partner. He ends up dead a few days later."

"I didn't...I would *never*...how could you..."

"I'm going to need you to come in," he went on smoothly. "I need to interrogate you myself."

"I've already been questioned," she told him. "You said you listened to the interview between Detective Warner and me. There's no other information that I have regarding Shelly and Ricky."

The detective was quiet.

"I'm sorry about Detective Warner, I really am," she continued. "But everyone is trying to pin all of these murders on me, and I refuse to let them. I'm innocent."

"And you believe that Tabatha Andrews is the one responsible for these murders," the detective said after a brief pause.

She hesitated before answering. She hadn't taken the time to think about who could have possibly killed Detective Warner. She'd assumed he had been killed in the line of duty.

"Fingerprints were found at the scene of the Kellerman murder, fingerprints belonging to Tabatha Andrews," the detective continued.

She gasped.

"I shouldn't be telling you this information because it's extremely sensitive information and we don't want the media to catch wind of it," the detective went on, "but for some reason I think I can trust you. After all, my partner did."

"So since her fingerprints were found at the scene, and Detective Warner knew this information, naturally you think…"

"That she killed my partner after he confronted her about it," the detective finished for her.

As disappointed as she was that she was still in Patty Coben's body, Tabatha had to admit that a small part of her was relieved that she was able to carry out her Halloween costume plan.

Shortly after her discussion with the detective, she removed a box of hair dye from one of her shopping bags from the previous night. She hadn't dyed her own hair in a long time; prior to switching bodies with Patricia Coben, she'd made frequent trips to the local hair salon and had her hair styled there. She probably hadn't dyed her hair since junior high school, but she could still clearly remember the steps that she needed to perform.

After what seemed like hours of bending over the kitchen sink, she took to drying and styling her long, dark locks.

Brendon was ripping and running throughout the house, on a soaring sugar high. He poked his head into the kitchen several times as she dyed her hair, but he rarely spoke. She hated to admit it, but the little booger was definitely growing on her. The more time she spent in this household, the more she could appreciate the family that resided there.

Sure, Mr. And Mrs. Coben seemed a little self-absorbed. They didn't have as much interest in their children's lives as they should, but they still loved their children. That much was obvious with how hard both parents worked. Brendon could be annoying at times, but little brothers were *supposed* to be annoying. And there was the rare occasion that he actually tried to be helpful.

She'd always wanted to have a little brother or sister, but her own parents didn't want to have more children. As a result, she'd been spoiled with attention whenever she'd wanted it. She'd had her father wrapped around her little finger and her mother couldn't stay angry with her for long. Her household was noticeably different from this one, but each household had its charm.

After drying her hair, she started to make her way upstairs when the doorbell rang. She could hear Brendon's footsteps darting down the stairs, but she called up to him, "I'll get the door."

He came to a halt at the last step and peered over the railing.

She pulled her hair into a topknot on top of her head and opened the front door. Standing on her front porch step was none other than Aidan Powers. She tried to hide her surprise and failed. "What are you doing here?" she demanded.

His bright blue eyes sparkled at her boldness. "I wish to speak with you."

"This isn't a good time."

"I can't think of a better time than now," he said softly. Without waiting for an invitation, he breezed past her and entered the living room of the Coben family's house.

She gawked at him for several moments before closing the front door and following him into the living room. "What do you want to talk to me about?"

"I wanted to give you a warning," he said without turning to face her. He surveyed his surroundings and seemed to appreciate the coziness of the place. With a gentle smile, he glanced over his shoulder at her. "I'm not certain, but I believe that tonight is the night that both of your fates will be decided."

She crossed her arms over her chest.

"I like your hair by the way," he said casually.

"When you say that tonight is the night that our fates will be decided...you mean, tonight is the night that we find out whether or not I'll be cursed to live in Patty Coben's body forever?" She approached him and jabbed an index finger into her own chest. "Because I followed the rules that were in that little book of yours and nothing happened when I woke up. I was still Patty Coben."

"Everything will unfold when it should," Aidan said cryptically. "And not one moment beforehand."

"I don't know what that means, Aidan!" she shouted. "You have a habit of talking in circles. Just be straight with me. Will I be forced to live life as Patty Coben?"

He shrugged his shoulders. "I don't have the power to decide your fate."

"You just have the power to stand by and watch?" she muttered under her breath.

One of his eyebrows lifted in askance.

"So you came by to give me a warning," she said, "and you've delivered the warning. Don't let the door hit you on the way out."

His laugh was as melodic as the tinkling of bells over his magic shop door. He moved towards the front door with his hands shoved into the pockets of neatly pressed slacks. "Just remember my warning," he said before leaving.

chapter twenty-six

"You look tense."

Zander nearly jumped out of his skin at the sound of the voice coming from behind him. He'd been nervously scanning the crowd, wanting to know the precise moment that Patty arrived. He bent to embrace her, careful not to get any creases or wrinkles in his long cape. He'd known that it had been cliché, but he had dressed up as a vampire.

Patty, with her sick sense of humor, had attended the party as a dead Homecoming Queen. She wore an elegant dress that had been deliberately tattered and shredded. Fake blood had been smeared along her arms and dripped down the corners of her mouth. A broken crown rested on her head, but her hair had been perfectly styled. Not many students would pick up on the relevance of this costume, but Zander definitely did. And he hated Patty all the more for it.

Music blasted from speakers that were positioned in the living room, and already the party was in full gear. Students danced with each other in the living room and stuffed their faces in the kitchen. Most of the students had been creative with their costumes. There were mummies, one other vampire that Zander knew of, a few werewolves, Lara Croft the Tomb Raider, and zombies. Brian and Freddy had shown up as the Super Mario Brothers. They'd conned a Vista Heights High sophomore into coming as Princess Peach. Everyone seemed to be having a good time, except the host.

Zander did admit that he was nervous. He didn't know how Patty would react to seeing the real Tabatha show up to the party. He didn't even know what Tabatha had dressed up as. Patty might not even recognize her, if they were lucky.

Patty was tugging on his arm now. She wanted him to dance with her. He pulled her against him and started shuffling his feet, but she didn't have his full attention. There was a heavy feeling in the pit of his stomach.

There was a commotion towards the foyer of his parents' house. It took awhile for him to notice, but several of the students were shouting. Some of the dancers cleared the floor to allow someone passage into the room.

Zander nearly tripped over his own feet. He looked down at the girl that he was dancing with, and he looked up again. It couldn't be possible, could it? Could there really be *two* Tabathas?

"Hi, Zander," the new girl said.

His eyes traveled down the length of her. Her hair was dark and styled to perfection. Her eyes were bright blue instead of dark brown, but that was the only flaw in the entire costume. She was dressed in a tight shirt and a short skirt. Her heels added about four inches to her height. Her legs appeared long and tan. Lip gloss shined on her lips. Eyeliner had been applied to her eyelids and mascara had been applied to her eyelashes. She appeared to be more gorgeous than she had ever been.

The girl in his arms finally seemed to notice that something was out of the ordinary. She stepped back and looked up at him; then she turned to look in the direction that he was looking. Her eyes widened and her breath caught in her throat. "What is this?" she shrieked.

The new girl did a slow turn. "Do you like my costume?"

"Who are you supposed to be?" Patty demanded.

"Well, I'm supposed to be *you*," came the expected answer.

All of the partygoers started talking at once. Several of them withdrew cell phones and took pictures of the two Tabathas confronting each other.

"You could never be me," Patty said through clenched teeth. "I'm one of a kind."

"And I should know," Tabatha shot back with a flip of her hair. "You still haven't told me what you think about my costume."

"I think you look ridiculous. And you're way too fat to be wearing that."

Brian pushed towards the front of the crowd. "I don't think she looks fat at all," he said, openly leering at the real Tabatha.

Patty scowled at him.

Tabatha flipped her long, dark hair over her shoulder. "Thank you, Brian."

"Oh, so you know me," Brian said, daring to throw an arm across her shoulder. "And here I don't know a thing about you. What's your name, cutie?"

Tabatha hesitated.

"Why don't you tell him what your name is?" Patty shouted. "Don't you think everyone should know who you *really* are?"

"I'm..." Tabatha started, blinking her eyes rapidly. "I'm..."

"Tell them!" Patty screamed at the top of her lungs.

Tabatha bowed her head and pursed her lips shut.

Patty's eyes grew cold. "You don't have the guts to tell everyone that you're Fatty Patty Coben?"

Gasps sounded throughout the crowd of teenagers.

Even Brian removed his arm from Tabatha's shoulders. "What?" he asked, sounding confused.

"Underneath all of that makeup and hair dye and self-tanner, she's still chunky, fat, flabby Patty Coben," Patty accused, pointing a slender index finger in Tabatha's direction.

"She might be Patty Coben, but I don't think we can call her Fatty Patty anymore," Freddy said from the crowd. "She looks *hot!*"

Tabatha blushed, but no one noticed because of the spray tan she'd applied earlier.

Patty stamped her foot and whirled around, disappearing through the crowd of high school students.

Zander still stood in the middle of the dance floor, looking dumbfounded. He wasn't sure if he could believe his eyes.

Tabatha smiled shyly at him.

Freddy yelled to the high school freshman behind the makeshift deejay booth, "Can we crank the music back up!"

The living room floor was immediately overflowing with a crowd of dancing teenagers. Some of the girls were still gossiping about what had just happened, but for the most part everyone wanted to get back to dancing and having fun.

Tabatha approached her boyfriend slowly. She took one of his hands in hers and started dancing. "I probably should have warned you about this," she said.

He nodded his head. "Yeah. A warning would have definitely been nice."

She laughed. "I'm sorry. I wanted to surprise you."

"You definitely did that. You surprised me and...everyone else here. I can't believe you came here as Tabatha."

"I came here as...myself."

"I know that, but not many other people know that."

She shrugged her shoulders. "I'm done caring about what other people think, Zander. I've spent my entire life worrying about what other people thought about me. I've spent my entire life wondering if I was cute enough or talented enough or smart enough or funny enough for everyone else. I never really took a step back and thought about what I wanted, or who I wanted to be."

Startled by her outburst, he said, "You were always perfect to me."

She smiled a smile that brightened up the entire room. "I know. And I never appreciated that, not until recently."

He pulled her against him and buried his head in her hair.

Patty stood in the upper hallway, leaning over a cherry wood railing. From where she stood, she could clearly see the living room. She could clearly see her classmates dancing and enjoying themselves. And in the midst of that crowd, she could clearly see Zander dancing with Tabatha. Her face grew hot. For the past few days, she'd suspected that Tabatha had gone to Zander and told him everything. She hadn't wanted to believe that to be true, but she noted how closely they were dancing together. She noticed how he wrapped his arms around Tabatha and pulled her closer to him.

If he thought I was Tabatha, he would have come running after me, she thought to herself. *He wouldn't have let me leave like that, not without making sure I was all right first.* Which led her to believe that he knew everything. And she couldn't allow him to ruin the life that she was making for herself. So she made the decision right then and there that she had to kill Zander and Tabatha. And tonight was the perfect night to do it.

chapter twenty-seven

After Patty made her dramatic exit, Tabatha finally took the time to admire the decorations that lined the walls and graced the floors. A six foot tall corpse had greeted her at the front door, holding his own head in his hands. It had been a statue of course, but it had looked so life-like, she hadn't known if it was a statue or one of her classmates in a very clever disguise. Spider-webs created frightening mazes in each corner of the room. Fake blood was splattered in various places, sometimes in the shape of handprints or footprints.

She wondered who had helped Zander get all of this together. Surely, he hadn't taken the time to decorate the place himself.

She looked at him now as he twirled her around on the living room floor. The furniture had been pushed against the walls to create a makeshift dance floor. Everyone seemed to be enjoying themselves. Freddy and Brian were comically dancing with each other, the ever humorous duo dressed in their Super Mario Brothers getups.

Despite the fact that Stephanie, Mary, and Dana were Patty's friends, Tabatha found herself wishing that they had attended tonight. The truth of the matter was that they had become her friends sometime within the past few weeks. After telling them who she really was, she'd expected them to treat her differently. After all, she was Tabatha the Terrible. She hadn't cared about anyone but herself and she'd been the one who had played a cruel prank on their friend. Shockingly enough, they had believed her and they'd even sympathized with her. Even beyond that, they'd been a great help to her for the past few weeks.

"What are you thinking about?" Zander was looking concerned, with his brows furrowed and his mouth slanted.

She shrugged her shoulders. "Everything," she answered vaguely. "Everything I've been through for the past few weeks. Everything I put Patty through."

"That's a lot of thinking," he commented.

She nodded her head. "Yeah."

"If we hadn't played that joke on her on the night of the Homecoming Dance, I don't think any of this would have happened," he said thoughtfully, looking at some point over her head.

"You're probably right," she agreed. "I wish I could take it all back, you know?"

He hugged her closer to him. He didn't know what to tell her. There was no way either of them could have known that their actions would have such extreme consequences. He wasn't using that as an excuse by any means, of course. Whether or not they could have foreseen the future, they should have never put Patty through the things that they had. If he'd known that her boyfriend had broken up with her only days before their horrible prank, there was no way he would have gone through with it. He hadn't really wanted to participate in the practical joke to begin with. After all, Patty had always been nice to him. She'd always seemed like a sweet girl, and she only seemed sweeter once he'd gotten to know her.

The lights flickered off. Then they flickered back on.

He blinked his eyes. Had he imagined that?

The CD that was playing skipped a few beats. The lights snapped off again. And chaos ensued.

A few freshmen girls screamed unnecessarily and Brian took advantage of the situation, always around to make fun of someone should the need arise. "Aww, do the little babies need a night light? I mean, come on. This is *obviously* something that our party host has rigged up. It is Halloween, after all."

The entire room was completely pitch-black. Zander couldn't see Brian, but he responded anyway. "I hate to disappoint you buddy, but this isn't my set-up."

"*Sure*, Zander," Brian said. "It's going to be a little more difficult to spook me, okay? I don't scare easily."

Zander started to repeat that the power outage hadn't been his idea, but his words died in his throat when a source of light became visible in the room.

It seemingly appeared out of nowhere, a dull red light that started off as a small speck on the floor in the center of the living room. The speck quickly grew until it was the size of a human person, and wrapped within its depths was a teenage girl with long, dark hair...a teenage girl who was dressed as a dead Homecoming Queen.

Freddy seemed to be the smartest of the bunch. He didn't hesitate before attempting to make a run for the door.

The dead Homecoming Queen lifted one of her hands, spread her fingers wide, and chanted a series of foreign-sounding words. A burst of energy shot forth from her hand, slamming the front door shut. The telltale clicking sound of locks traveled into the living room. Freddy could be heard struggling at the door, trying with all of his might to get the door open. It wouldn't budge.

Zander's arm tightened around Tabatha's shoulders.

"Don't you two look like the most adorable couple?" Patty asked silkily, seeming to float towards them. Her long, dark hair trailed behind her. The strange red glow didn't fade; it only grew brighter, surrounding her within its confines.

"You don't know how sorry I am for what I did to you," Tabatha said softly.

Patty's eyes locked with hers. Her mouth twisted into a smirk. "You think I want your apology?" she demanded. "I don't want an apology from you. We're past the point of apologizing."

"I'm still sorry," Tabatha said again.

"We both are," Zander chimed in.

"I'm not even going to start with you yet," Patty said between clenched teeth, directing these words at Zander.

"If I had known that Ricky had dumped you-" Tabatha began.

"Don't even *think* Ricky's name," Patty whispered, cutting the other girl off. She closed her eyes and pursed her lips shut. When she opened her eyes again, fire leapt within their depths.

"What would Ricky think if he could see you now?" Tabatha asked bravely. "What would Shelly think? Huh? And how about Aidan? What would *he* think about you abusing the magic that he gave to you?"

Patty stretched out both of her arms and roughly shoved Tabatha to the floor. She bent over the other girl with a cruel look in her eyes. "You silly, silly girl," she said softly. "The magic I'm using is ten times more powerful than anything Aidan could have ever shown me."

Locked in the back room of his shop, Aidan somberly witnessed what was unfolding at Zander Davis's house.

"You silly, silly girl," the image of Patty was saying. *"The magic I'm using is ten times more powerful than anything Aidan could have ever shown me."*

Aidan caused the images to disappear with a dismissive wave of his hand. He casually removed the long, dark robe from his shoulders and prepared to leave his shop. "Is that what you think, Patty?" he wondered aloud.

It had finally dawned on most of the party guests that what was happening wasn't a joke or a prank or a clever set-up in honor of the macabre holiday. They seemed to absorb the fact that the argument occurring before them was genuine. They started to inch towards the door, where

Freddy had long since given up. He was sitting on the floor with his back pressed against the door.

Brian knelt down so that he could speak to his friend. "If I die and you make it out of here alive, Freddy, you can have my stereo," he said earnestly. Then he added, almost as an afterthought, "You'll have to break into my room and steal it though, because I already promised it to my little sister awhile back."

Tabatha hadn't made an effort to stand up. She remained stretched out across the floor. She was vaguely aware of her boyfriend kneeling down by her side. He pulled her into a sitting position and kept asking if she was okay. Couldn't he hear her? Couldn't he hear that she was answering that yes, she was fine? She just had the wind knocked out of her, that's all.

It apparently didn't please Patty to see Zander rushing to Tabatha's aid, because she yanked Zander up by the collar of his black and red cape. He was startled at how strong she was. She should have never been able to lift him off of the ground. He weighed nearly double what she weighed.

Still, she plucked him up as if she were plucking up a light, fluffy pillow. Then, with just as little effort, she hurled him across the room.

Their classmates couldn't believe their eyes. Several of the girls were crying at this point, wanting nothing more than the chance to escape from this house alive. They didn't know the specifics of what was happening and they were sure they didn't *want* to know. Still, the door would not budge. The locks were engaged and no one knew how to disengage them.

Meanwhile, Patty stalked across the room to where Zander had fallen. After cruelly kicking him in the stomach, she dropped down to the floor and brushed his hair out of his eyes. "Tabatha and I had the same gym period, and sometimes our classes shared the gym and the pool. She used to love making fun of me in gym class." She continued playing with Zander's hair as memories clouded her eyes.

"Did you know that whenever we had to swim for gym class, I would make sure that I was the first one into the pool and the last one out of the pool?"

He was in and out of consciousness, but everyone else seemed to be listening to the story.

She went on. "I had to be the first one in the pool and the last one out, you see. If I wasn't, then everyone would see me in my swimsuit. I always wanted to wear a t-shirt over my swimsuit, but our gym teacher wouldn't let me. She made me wear that skimpy little one-piece swimsuit and I never felt comfortable in it. And Tabatha and her friends always made fun of me when they saw me in it. They laughed at me and said horrible, hateful things."

Tears formed in Tabatha's eyes. She struggled to stand on her feet.

"And I don't want you to apologize," Patty said quickly. "I've heard you apologize more than enough. Apologies won't bring Ricky back. They won't bring Shelly back, or Detective Warner back. They're all dead, and they're dead for good. And me...I'm changed for good. I'll never be the same girl that I was." The red glow seemed to fade away a little bit as she bowed her head.

"It's never too late," Tabatha whispered.

Patty's head lifted. "What do you mean?" she asked. "I've killed three people! There's no turning back from that. Three people are dead because of me...and because of you."

Tabatha grew tense at those words.

Patty tilted her head to the side. "You had to be aware of the fact that if you hadn't played that stupid prank on me, we wouldn't be in this situation. I'm sure that occurred to you."

"Yes, it did," Tabatha admitted.

"Good. Then you're not as stupid as I thought you were." Patty took a deep breath and glanced around her. Her gaze halted on the group of students that was clustered near the front door. With a roll of her eyes, she lifted one of her hands and disengaged the locks.

The teenagers didn't hesitate in flooding out of the house as soon as the door was pulled open.

Detective Jack Goldenstein carefully approached the Davis family residence. Tabatha had given him the address during their phone conversation earlier that day. She'd explained that there would be a Halloween party happening at this address. She hadn't explained much more than that. He didn't know if she was under the impression another murder was going to take place. She'd simply told him the address and informed him that he might want to make a guest appearance.

So here he was, creeping up to the house as quietly as possible, with his hand hiding beneath the inside of his jacket in case he had to draw his gun for some reason. He didn't know what to expect, but surely it wasn't a stampede of teenagers running out of the front door of the house and down the porch steps, as if they were being chased from some monster from a horror movie.

He saw goblins, ghouls, rock stars, and video game characters. These teenagers hadn't spared any expense when it had come to putting together their Halloween costumes. That much was apparent as they made as if to run past him.

He grabbed the arm of the nearest student. "What is going on in there?" he questioned.

The teenager, who was dressed up as Super Mario, shook his head. "You don't want to know man, trust me on this."

Jack withdrew his badge from the inside of his coat pocket. "Try me."

The kid's eyes grew round. "You're a cop?"

"I'm Detective Goldenstein. I need to know what is going on inside that house."

"Some girl in there is flipping out, man!" the kid exclaimed. He removed the red cap from his head and glanced towards the house. "And I don't just mean going crazy. There's some weird stuff going on in there. There's this weird red light. And all of the power went out. And she keeps talking about when she used to be fat, but she's Tabatha Andrews. I've never known Tabatha Andrews to be fat, man. I don't know. It's really weird in there."

"Thanks, kid." The detective ran towards the porch, no longer concerned about being as quiet and stealthy as he could be. The front door had been left open, so he didn't have to worry about breaking and entering.

There was a light touch at his shoulder that caused him to nearly jump out of his skin, though. With wide eyes, he arched a look over his shoulder.

He wasn't sure if the person he was looking at was a man or a woman. The person he was looking at had long, platinum blonde hair and strange-looking, light blue eyes. When the person spoke, he could be sure that he was looking at a man, but only once the person started speaking could he even be remotely sure.

"I'm not sure if you want to enter this house," a gentle deep voice warned him.

"I'm not sure you should even be here," the detective countered. "What are you dressed up as?"

"I'm not dressed up," the man said, glancing over the detective's shoulder. "But I am sure that you do not want to enter this house, not now."

The dark-haired detective flashed his badge again. "I'm here on account of my partner, who's no longer with us," he said. "Not that I have to explain my reasoning to you. I have business here."

The slender man shrugged his shoulders. "I also have business here."

"It looks like we're both going in, then," Detective Goldenstein announced.

"Yes," the other man agreed.

chapter twenty*eight

"I'm glad you let everyone else go," Tabatha said. "This is just between you and me."

"And don't forget Zander," Patty reminded, standing up from where she'd knelt next to the unconscious boy she'd thrown across the room only moments before.

"Zander isn't in this."

"Zander is very *much* in this," Patty argued. "He was a sucker for a pretty face. He pretended to like me because you wanted him to."

Tabatha started to speak, but she was cut off.

"I don't want to hear it. He's not a five year old kid. He is accountable for his own actions. I don't care how pretty you are or were. He should have been able to stand up for what he believed in, instead of playing along with your sick and twisted games." Patty closed the distance between Tabatha and herself. "I'm not going to let him off the hook just because he's suddenly okay with dating someone who looks like Fatty Patty Coben. He will suffer just as you will suffer." With those words, the eerie red glow surrounding her seemed to brighten.

Tabatha started backing away from the dead Homecoming Queen. Then, she turned around, intent on running away. But there was nowhere to run. A large, picture window was in front of her. There was nowhere for her to go. She could see her reflection clearly in the clear glass. She could also see Patty's reflection approaching hers.

Both girls froze at the exact same instant, dazed by how similar their reflections were. If it weren't for the difference in their Halloween costumes, they probably wouldn't have been able to tell one reflection apart from the other.

"It's a shame, really, how superficial people are," Patty said softly. "Everyone talks about how important it is to be an individual and how great it is to be different from everyone else. That's the mumbo jumbo they teach us. But when we get older, we're expected to conform to society's ideas of *beautiful*."

"I'm sorry for what Zander and I did to you," Tabatha said.

"I told you that I don't want to hear apologies."

"You didn't let me finish," Tabatha said, looking Patty's reflection in the eye. "I'm sorry for what Zander and I did to you. You probably don't believe me, but I truly am. Even though I'm sorry for what we did, though, you can't blame Zander and I for everything you've done."

Patty frowned.

"Yes, we played a very cruel joke on you. And yes, that joke came at a very difficult time in your life, because of the fact that you and Ricky broke up a few days before that. Some horrible things happened to you, Patty, and for that I'm sorry. But you should know right from wrong." Without warning, she spun around to face the dead Homecoming Queen. "Killing people is *wrong*, Patty. It's *wrong*. And as much as you try, you can't blame Zander and me for that. You took it upon yourself to kill people who were getting in the way of what you wanted. Sooner or later, you're going to have to admit that to yourself."

Patty's eyes, which had held so much emotion only moments before, turned as cold as ice. "I wouldn't be this way if it weren't for you," she said in a voice so chilly, it knocked the temperature of the room down several degrees.

"Maybe you wouldn't have gone completely nuts if it weren't for us," Tabatha said, "but maybe you would have. I don't know about that. But what I do know is that it's never too late to do the right thing. And you can turn everything around right now. Look at Zander. *Look* at him."

Patty glanced towards where Zander was sprawled out on the floor. He'd lost consciousness quite awhile ago and hadn't opened his eyes since.

"He needs a hospital, Patty."

Patty tilted her head to the side. "So do you, Tabs."

Tabatha's brows furrowed in confusion. "What do you mean?"

Patty started murmuring a string of words too low for Tabatha to hear. She chanted the words over and over again.

Tabatha felt a gentle push at her chest, but Patty hadn't touched her. She clasped her hands to her chest, trying in vain to back away from the other girl. There was nowhere else for her to go. Her back was flat against the window.

Patty continued to mumble the unfamiliar words over and over again. She raised her arms over her head, and the glow that surrounded her became a blinding light.

The gentle force that Tabatha felt against her chest intensified, and she felt herself being shoved through the glass window. A rush of wind swept around her as she flew through the air. She blinked once, and then twice. She saw the open night sky as she thudded heavily against the ground outside of the Davis family's living room window. Small cuts lined her arms.

She could feel the grass beneath her back. It was difficult for her to breathe. It felt like there was a heavy weight pressing down on her chest. It felt like her chest was caving in. She turned her head to the right and saw two figures entering the house. She tried to call out to them, but her voice wasn't much more than a whisper.

She could clearly hear the sounds of cars driving past the house, of some of the neighbors' kids carrying on about how much candy they'd gotten while trick or treating. She could hear the sound of the wind rustling the crisp leaves on the trees hanging overhead. Somewhere, a siren gave a shrill cry. Or maybe it was a car alarm, she couldn't tell. All sound was starting to die down. The sounds of the night were sharp one moment, and non-existent the next. And then her vision started to fade, too. The last thing she caught a glimpse of was the night sky, cloudless and studded with a gazillion of twinkling stars.

Her second-to-last thought was of Zander. She hoped that he was okay, that he got the medical attention that he needed. He'd looked to be in bad shape, and he had tried so hard to protect her. Hopefully Patty got everything that was coming to her.

Her very last thought was of the pamphlet, and its final step. The final step had instructed her to sleep, and as heavy as her eyelids felt, she wouldn't have trouble following those instructions.

Even though her eyes were still open, she couldn't see anything. She could no longer hear anything. She could no longer think anything. Tabatha Andrews was no longer of this world.

When Aidan and Detective Goldenstein entered the house, the girl who *appeared* to be Tabatha Andrews was standing over Zander Davis. There was a thick red mist that clouded around her.

Aidan was quick to act. He stepped forward. "Leave him alone, Patty."

Patty didn't lift her gaze from Zander's face. "But he hurt me," she said numbly. "He hurt me and he has to pay for that."

"That isn't for you to decide, my dear," Aidan said, drawing nearer and nearer to the girl. "You have dabbled in the black arts, and you have gotten in way over your head, I'm afraid."

"I couldn't risk going back to what I was," she mumbled.

"What was so wrong with what you were?" he asked her. "What you were was a young, cheerful, caring girl who charmed everyone around her. There were some tough times, but everyone has those. Life isn't easy. It was never meant to be easy. There are ups and there are downs. There are times when it seems everyone loves us. There are times when it seems that no one at all loves us. Things can go from good to bad to worse to good again, all in the span of a couple of days. Such is life."

"I've taken the lives of others," she said. "It's too late for me."

He slid a hand beneath her chin and tilted her face up. "It's never too late, Patty. Do you hear me?"

The red glow surrounding her faded, nearly to the point of disappearing. Tears slid down her cheeks and she didn't meet his eyes for several minutes.

The detective perked at the fact that Aidan had called the girl Patty, but he didn't want to jump into the conversation. Not yet.

"I want to repeat that it's never too late for someone to turn around, but I will have to bind you from using magic," Aidan explained matter-of-factly. "I told you to use the wares that I gave you without malice and without ill-intent. You have failed to do that, and since you've failed to do that, I am forced to forbid you to use magic of any kind ever again."

Her eyes met his, and they were empty. Soulless. "I won't let you do that," she challenged in her soft voice.

"Where is the other girl?" the detective finally asked, unable to withhold his question for much longer.

Patty didn't take her eyes off of Aidan. "I've taken care of her."

Aidan's jaw twitched, but otherwise there was no reaction to those words. He launched into his own chant. The lights flickered on for a moment. The song that had been playing on the stereo earlier blasted from the speakers. The floor beneath their feet trembled beneath the weight of his power.

For the first time, Patty appeared to be frightened. "I thought you wanted to help me!" she screamed.

"Precisely," he said. "I wanted to help you. I didn't want to assist with creating a cruel, heartless wretch."

As the detective drew closer to the broken window, Aidan continued his chanting. Patty screamed for him to stop. She begged for him to stop. She tugged at the sleeve of his jacket. He refused to stop chanting, and once she realized this, she ran at him full force, intending to knock him down.

Still chanting, he disappeared into thin air. She could still hear his voice, and so could the detective, but Aidan was nowhere to be found. She tripped over an empty soda can that one of the students had dropped and fell to the floor. A cotton candy pink compact was located six inches ahead of her. She could see her reflection in the mirror from where she'd fallen.

The lights flickered on and off, as did the music playing on the stereo. As the lights flickered, so did her image in the mirror. It seemed at times, she could see who she truly was, Patricia Coben, with her dirty blonde hair and chubby cheeks. At random intervals though, Tabatha's tanned face and dark hair would replace the image of the face she'd been born with.

Aidan materialized again, still chanting the binding spell. He was binding her from being able to use magic and he was binding her from being able to cause harm to other people and herself.

She could hear his voice chanting in her head, but all she could do was focus on the image of the dark-haired girl in the mirror. She'd been through a lot tonight. She'd done a lot of bad things tonight. But that was all right, wasn't it? Because no matter how bad she'd been, no matter how much she misbehaved…boy, was she pretty. And who couldn't forgive such a pretty face?

epilogue

The funeral was a simple ceremony. The Halloween party from last week was still the talk of the town. There were many questions and not many answers. Why had Patty Coben dressed up as Tabatha for Halloween? Where had Tabatha run off to? She hadn't been spotted for nearly a week now. Why had Tabatha gone crazy at the party and what had she been babbling about? How did Zander fit into all of this? The questions went on forever.

Zander, perched in a wheelchair, watched the funeral with tears filling his eyes. He'd loved Tabatha with all of his heart, and he had failed to protect her. He was sure there was something else he could have done. For starters, he definitely shouldn't have thrown the party, not after finding out what was really going on. And he, like the rest of Vista Heights High, also wondered where Tabatha was. She'd disappeared after the night of the party. No one had seen her or heard from her since.

His eyes locked on the polished oak casket as it was lowered into the ground. He could hear two older women talking in hushed tones. They were seated somewhere behind him, whispering and gossiping to each other.

"It's a shame, really. I used to baby-sit the Coben girl and she always used to be so bubbly and funny and full of life. She always looked for the bright side of things, you know? She didn't like to dwell on the negative. She always had friends around and she was so outgoing."

"Did you hear about the other girl?" the second lady asked. "You know, the one who disappeared?"

"Her name was Tatiana or something, right?" the first lady questioned.

"That's right," the second lady answered.

"Well I don't know much about her," the first lady said, "but I did hear that she was a pretty girl."

"Very pretty indeed," the second lady confirmed.

Zander closed his eyes, trying to block out their words.

Detective Goldenstein stopped by the Vista Heights Psychiatric Care Facility in hopes of questioning their newest patient: Tabatha Andrews. The night of the Davis boy's Halloween party, she'd been taken into custody and held at the county jail. During the days following, though, her family's lawyer did everything within his power to have her moved to the psychiatric care facility.

Aesthetically speaking, the room wasn't much better than a jail cell. A narrow bed was pressed against the far wall. A barred window overlooked a gray metal desk. The only other piece of furniture in the room was a rickety, old vanity. The family must have somehow convinced the facility to furnish the room with a vanity, because none of the other rooms in the place had one.

The teenager with the long, dark hair sat at the vanity and continually brushed her hair, staring into space and mumbling to no one in particular. The detective couldn't tell if she was trying to use the magic that Aidan had spoken of the night of the Halloween party, or if she was simply talking to herself.

When he tried to engage her in a conversation, it seemed that she was looking right *through* him. She didn't even acknowledge his presence.

She returned to her lovely mirror and said, as if to herself, "I've done a lot of bad things, some very bad things. But I'll be able to go home soon, do you know why?" She paused as she continued to brush her hair. "I'll be able to go home soon, because I'm so pretty. They wouldn't keep such a pretty girl in a place like this. I'm so pretty, they'll let me go with barely a slap on the wrist. And everyone will forget all of the bad things I've done, and I can go back to being me...except I *won't* be me, because I've killed me." She shook her head and looked up to the ceiling.

The detective folded his arms across his chest, feeling an immense amount of pity for the girl.

"But wait a minute. I couldn't have killed me, because I'm right here. So I must have killed someone else...but who else could I have killed? I'm getting so confused. Oh dear, dear, dear, I'm getting confused. I killed me, but I didn't kill me. How is that possible?"

The detective turned and left the room. The orderly who'd led him to the room closed the door and locked it.

"She's been that way for awhile," the orderly said, brushing locks of his red hair out of his eyes. "She just keeps talking in circles. We don't know what to make of it sometimes."

The detective didn't respond, even though he *did* know what to make of the girl's confusing babble.

The orderly rambled on, "I can't imagine actually having to interrogate her. She didn't know up from down when she came in."

The detective continued to watch the teenager through the small window in the heavy steel door. She'd brushed her hair so much that there were several bald patches forming on each side of her head.

The orderly clucked his tongue. "It's a shame, really, that she's in a place like this. I mean, she's so young and pretty. You know?"

The detective placed a pair of sunglasses over his eyes. "Yeah," he said, shoving his hands into the pockets of his slacks and leaving the orderly behind to gaze after the dark-haired girl who only appeared to be Tabatha Andrews.

Sneak Preview of
Hidden Treasures:
Willow Weeping

Willow Weeping artwork by Il Sun Jung

❁❁❁❁❁❁❁❁❁❁❁❁❁❁❁❁❁❁❁❁❁❁❁❁❁❁❁❁❁❁❁

They'd been in the car for so long, that the windows were starting to fog up. Abigail Harrington leaned forward and wiped at the foggy window with the sleeve of her sweatshirt. For a brief moment, she could see her family's house, perched at the end of a narrow driveway. It was a cute, two-story house that had been painted several colors before her parents had decided on a light blue color. It didn't take long for the fog to settle on the glass again, causing the image of her family's house to fade.

Seated beside her was Jason Prescott, the boy she'd been dating for the past two years. He was tall and lanky with neatly cut blonde hair. His eyes were bright blue and fringed with lashes that seemed too long and thick for a boy. Whenever he turned those eyes on her, goosebumps always prickled along her forearms.

He turned those eyes on her now and looked at her for a long moment. She couldn't imagine how she looked. She hadn't bothered styling her hair, so the long, dark strands hung limply down her back. She hadn't put any makeup on, and she hadn't made an effort to dress up.

Why would she make an effort to look cute for him, when this was probably the last time that she was going to see him?

The silence was almost deafening. She didn't know how much more of it she could take. She turned and made as if to open the passenger side door.

"Abby, wait," he said, settling a hand on her shoulder.

She arched a look at him over her shoulder.

"Don't go, not yet."

"There's nothing left to say," she told him. "I'm not good at goodbyes, so let's just leave things where they are."

Even though she hadn't made an effort to dress up, he had. He was wearing a gray button-down dress shirt and a pair of dark slacks. Her friends called him "Prep" because of the way he dressed. His family had a lot of money and they didn't try to hide that fact. Jason wore expensive clothes and drove an expensive sports car.

As clean-cut as he was, she still liked him. He was fun to be around. He wasn't as squeaky-clean as he appeared to be, and she liked the fact that there was more than one side to him.

"What are you thinking?" he asked suddenly.

She shrugged her shoulders. "About how much I'm going to miss you."

"I'm going to miss you too, Abby," he said softly. "I wish your family didn't have to move. I thought we were going to graduate high school together, go to college together and move in with each other."

"That was the plan," she muttered, glaring through the fog at her family's house. A For Sale sign had been staked in their front yard, and several days ago someone had slapped a Sold sticker across the words "for sale." Her parents had found a buyer for their house, and they would be moving to Ohio.

"You'll still keep the same cell phone number, right?" he asked. "We can still talk to each other on the phone, and I can e-mail you."

"It won't be the same," she said moodily.

He sat back in his seat and stared at her. "I don't know what to say."

"Just say that you won't forget me," she whispered.

"What did you say? I didn't hear you."

"Nothing," she said, swiping at the tears that were starting in her eyes. "Could you walk me to my front door?"

He hopped out of the car and opened the door for her. Then, he walked her to the front door with his hands shoved down into his front pockets. He genuinely seemed to be at a loss for words and that wasn't like him.

Once they reached the front door, she turned to face him and stood on her tip-toes with her arms outstretched.

He leaned down and collected her in a hug. He allowed her to bury her face in his neck. "It's going to be okay," he promised.

"No it's not!" she cried, letting the tears come now. "I hate that we have to move. My family is so *stupid* sometimes. My dad is moving because of a job that's out in Ohio, but there are a lot of jobs here in Chicago. My parents are so selfish. They only care about themselves."

"Maybe your dad found a really good job out there," he reasoned.

She stepped away from him. "You're taking their side?"

"No," he hurried to say. "But they love you. I'm sure there's a reason why they're picking up and taking off to Ohio."

"Yeah, there's a reason," she muttered. "Because they're selfish. They could have at least waited until the end of my junior year!"

"Well I'll be around if you want to talk to me," he told her. "Just don't lose my number. I won't lose yours."

She hugged him again, and pressed a kiss to his lips.

They pressed their foreheads together and smiled wistfully at each other. "I love you, Abby," he whispered.

"I love you, too," she whispered back.

This was it. This was when they would tell each other goodbye. This was when he would talk down the sidewalk and speed off in his little sports car. This was the last time she would see him.

His arms were tight around her, but they started to loosen. She could feel him pulling away from her and she desperately wanted to cling to him. He brushed back a wayward strand of dark hair from her forehead, and she had never seen a smile so sad in her life.

"Ohio isn't *that* far, right?" he asked rhetorically. "We might be able to see each other during holidays and on some weekends."

"Sure," she agreed. A temporary flicker of hope shined in her eyes, but it quickly died out. She doubted her parents would ever allow her to borrow the car so she could make a four- or five-hour drive to see him. And even though he already had a car he could use, he would get swallowed up in parties and sports and he would forget about her.

They hugged one last time, and then she had to watch him leave. The tears *really* started flowing then. She offered a wave as he got into his flashy, blue sports car. Then he pulled away from the curb and all she could see of him was a twin set of taillights.

She wiped at both of her eyes, tried to get rid of the sniffles, and then stuck her hand out so that she could open the front door to her family's house.

Before she touched the doorknob, though, the door swung open on its own.

Shiloh Sanders is the pseudonym for Starr Sanders, who was born in Waco, Texas, and raised in Zion, Illinois. She has been writing short stories ever since she was a child and has been writing novels ever since junior high school. She currently writes in the genres of horror fiction, suspense, romance, young adult horror, and young adult suspense. In addition to *Hidden Treasures: Switched,* she has also written a horror fiction novel called *BloodLust: The Beginning* and a romance novel called *Open Book.* She still resides in Illinois and enjoys reading, spending time with family and friends, and scary movies.

This author can be contacted at: authorshilohsanders@yahoo.com
Author's website: www.starrsanders.com